The Wall Reader

the wall reader and other stories

ARLEN HOUSE – THE WOMEN'S PRESS

© Fiona Barr, Soinbhe Lally, Maureen O'Connor, Hilda Murphy, Harriet O'Carroll, Catherine Slattery, Bernadette Quinn, Mary Rose Callaghan and Arlen House – The Women's Press, 1979.

The publishers gratefully acknowledge the assistance of the Arts Council in the publication of this book.

Cover design by Deirdre Cullen,
from the screenprint 'Menses' by Irene Plazewska

ISBN 0 905223 10 1

Typesetting by Redsetter Ltd., Dublin.
Printed by Litho Press Co., Midleton, Co. Cork.
Published by Arlen House – The Women's Press, 2 Strand Road, Dublin 13.

preface

I am confident that readers will extend to these stories the welcome customarily reserved for new talent. There are risks and triumphs in these ten accounts of contemporary life which are, of course, nothing the same as those to be found in the finished statements of experienced writers.

That said, these new voices need no apology. The stories they tell are full of change, colour, force. If few of them — because of the circumstances of this competition which debarred writers already published — are technically perfect, still none of them have the false symmetry of the formula. If some of them are almost naked in their exposure of the fantasies of women in this country at this time, so much the better. It removes them from the couture conventions of the woman's magazine. For any new writer the greatest temptation is to alter their experience according to the most persuasive convention of the day. For women starting to write fiction the persuasion and the temptation exists in those increasingly sophisticated flatteries and reassurances which sell in magazines for women.

The best of these stories and the best in them suggests something quite opposite: that the truth of a woman's experience needs only art, not artifice, to make it compelling. In stories such as "The Wall-Reader" and "Underwear" in this anthology — to mention only two — there are preliminary excursions into private worlds that are far from reassuring. Those journeys into doubt and flux, which are to be found in one form or other, in almost all the stories amply justify this collection.

But there is in a sense a dimension to this book that is almost more exciting. Read together these stories hint at something very like a new force that could release new energies into the Irish short story. These ten accounts of disappointment, adventure, self-realization have tones and colours that could hardly have been projected twenty years ago in Ireland. There are impatiences and angers here that are new. Of themselves these do not make art, but they make the energy that augurs well for art.

Not that I am suggesting anything as simple or as simplified as the New Woman. But I think it could well be that the new expression of the old dilemmas will have a radical effect on this and other forms.

Having said this, I have an instinctive sympathy with the person for whom these are not sufficient justifications for the publication of this book, who has the uneasy feeling that writing by women only is writing only for women. Not so. The dilemmas and struggles outlined in these stories are human first and only then feminine.

I mention this because I am not only tolerant of the unease in that attitude; to a great extent I share it. I am convinced that the greatest enemy to excellent writing by women is the concept — gathering force in some quarters — of 'the woman writer'. The first implies the marvellous arrival among its peers of a new mode of perception and expression; the second only an extension, by its complicity with a minority status, of all the repressions and silences that have gone before.

I am confident that the energies and aspirations in these stories, as well as the standards by which they were judged, have protected them from this second category.

But why then a short story competition exclusively for women and under the auspices of a press such as Arlen House, which has a particular commitment to their interests? There can only be a contradiction here if there is any suspicion that the criteria by which talent is fostered are those by which it is judged.

Historically the condition of women in the arts has been one of a disproportionate silence. It is a mystery, it is a tragedy, but so it is. For that reason, it is surely not only permissible but imperative to encourage self-expression in the community of women — even if to do so means one must go about it in an organized, even an artificial way. I see only the same devices of protection in this as are employed every day in the protection of an industry, or the rotation of an unyielding acre.

These artifices of encouragement only become suspect and self-defeating if they influence the method of assessment, if the process, so to speak, is allowed to determine the product. As a judge, with Mary Lavin and David Marcus, I know how clearly the distinction was drawn.

Each of these stories was judged solely by the formal and stylistic criteria of the short story. Where these were relaxed at all it was because the verve and force of a new voice occasionally dragged the form out of shape. When that happened, a certain allowance was made for that sundering of form and substance which is the mark, indeed, almost the prerogative of new talent. Never, it should almost go without saying, was a consciousness of the sex of the writers a factor in the final, aesthetic decision.

Therefore, by the lights of this argument, I see an instructive distinction between this competition and the anthology which has emerged from it. The first belongs to that legitimate ploy of encouragement which is due to any community in which one suspects an inverse proportion of energy to expression. It has been generously sponsored by Maxwell House and the size of the entry alone suggests a vitality that should be sustained by this fosterage.

The anthology on the other hand is part of the more exacting search with which the future of good writing, not just good writing by women, is crucially involved. It is this search with which Arlen House, and all presses like it in Britain and America, has associated itself. It is motivated by the belief that there is an excellence of perception and expression latent in the community of women, and that as long as it lies dormant it is a wasting asset, to everyone, not just to one part of a society.

Only by the discovery of that excellence can the invidious concept of 'the woman writer' be banished. Only by the publication of it can the aims of a woman's press be accomplished: which are, not to feminize literature but to publish those writings which so humanize the feminine experience that they restore it, articulate and radical, to the total community to which it belongs, and which it has impoverished by its silence.

These stories are part of that excursion into silence. They are also fresh, entertaining, often poignant accounts of a private adventure. They tell a story and they tell it well. On all of these grounds, I commend them to the reader.

Eavan Boland

contents

PREFACE *by Eavan Boland*

the wall reader

Fiona Barr

'Shall only our rivers run free?' The question jumped out from the cobbled wall in huge white letters, as *The Peoples'* taxi swung round the corner at Beechmount.

'Looks like paint is running freely enough down here,' she thought to herself, as other slogans glided past in rapid succession. Reading Belfast's grim graffiti had become an entertaining hobby for her, and, she often wondered, was it in the dead of night that groups of boys huddled round a paint tin daubing walls and gables with tired political slogans and clichés? Did anyone ever see them? Was the guilty brush ever found? The brush is mightier than the bomb, she declared inwardly, as she thought of how celebrated among journalists some lines had become.

'Is there a life before death?'

Well, no one had answered that one yet, at least, not in this city.

The shapes of Belfast crowded in on her as the taxi rattled over the ramps outside the fortressed police barracks. Dilapidated houses, bricked-up terraces, splintered chaos and amputated life, rosy-cheeked soldiers, barely out of school,

1

and quivering with high-pitched fear. She thought of the thick-lipped youth who came to hi-jack the car, making his point by showing his revolver under his anorak, and of the others, jigging and taunting every July, almost sexual in their arrogance and hatred. Meanwhile, passengers climbed in and out at various points along the road, manoeuvering between legs, bags of shopping and umbrellas. The taxi swerved blindly into the road. No Highway Code here. As the woman's stop approached, the taxi swung up to the pavement, and she stepped out.

She thought of how she read walls – like tea-cups – and she smiled to herself. Pushing her baby in the pram to the supermarket, she had to pass under a motorway bridge that was peppered with lines, some in irregular lettering with the paint dribbling down the concrete, others written with felt-tip pens in minute secretive hand. A whole range of human emotions splayed itself with persistent anarchy on the walls. Messages: 'Ring me at eight, don't be late'; declarations: 'Two bob and she's yours'; exclamations: 'Man. Utd. are fab'; political jabs: 'Orange squash – great', and notes of historical import: '3rd Tank Regiment wuz here'. Oh how she longed to linger under the bridge taking each wall in turn, studying the meanest scrawl, pondering sensitivity, evaluating character, identifying subconscious fears, analysing childhoods.

'One could do worse than be a reader of walls', she thought, twisting Frost's words. Instead, though, the pram was rushed past the intriguing mural ('murial' as they call it here) with much gusto. Respectable housewives don't read walls!

Her husband had arrived home early today because of a bomb scare in work, as he explained. Despite the bombings which had propelled Northern Ireland onto the world's screens and newspapers, most people regarded these episodes as a fact of life now; tedious, disruptive at times and only of interest when fatalities occurred. The 'Troubles' as they were euphemistically named, remained for this couple as a remote, vaguely irritating wart on their life. They were simply an ordinary (she often groaned at the oppressive banality of the word), middle-class, family — hoping the baby would marry a doctor thereby raising them in their autumn days to the select legions of the upper-class.

Each day their lives followed the same routine — no harm in that sordid little detail, she thought. It helps structure one's existence. He went to the office, she fed the baby, washed the rapidly growing mound of nappies, prepared the dinner and looked forward to the afternoon walk. She had convinced herself she was happy with her lot, and yet felt disappointed at the pangs of jealousy endured on hearing of a friend's glamorous job or another's academic and erudite husband. If only someone noticed her from time to time, or even wrote her name on a wall declaring her existence worthwhile, 'A fine mind' or 'I was once her lover'. That way, at least, she would have evidence that she was making an impact on others.

That afternoon she dressed the baby and started out for her walk. 'Fantasy time' her husband called it, 'Wall-reading time', she knew it to be. On this occasion, however, she decided to avoid those concrete temptations and, instead, visit the park. Out along the main road, she pushed the pram, pausing to gaze into the hardware store's window, hearing the whine of the saracen as it thundered by, waking the baby and making her feel uneasy. A foot patrol of soldiers strolled past, their rifles, lethal even in the brittle sunlight of this March day, lounged lovingly and relaxed in the arms of their men. One soldier stood nonchalantly, almost impertinently, against a corrugated railing and stared at her. She always blushed when she passed troops. 'Locked up in barracks with no women', she had told her husband. (He remarked that she had a dirty mind). Hurrying out of the range of his eyes and possible sniper fire, she swung downhill out onto Stockman's Lane and into Musgrave Park.

The park is ugly, stark and hostile. Even in summer when courting couples seek out secluded spots, like mating cats, they reject Musgrave. There are a few trees, clustered together, standing like skeletons ashamed of their nakedness. The rest is grass, a green wasteland speckled with puddles of gulls squawking over a worm patch. The park is bordered by a hospital which has a military wing guarded by an army billet. The beauty of the place is its silence. It has only this. And here silence means peace. Horror, pain, terror do not exist within these railings. Belfast is beyond their boundaries, and past the frontiers of the eagerly forgetful imagination.

The hill up to the park bench was not the precipice it seemed, but the baby and pram were heavy. Ante-natal self-indulgence had taken its toll — her midriff was now most definitely a bulge . With one final push, pram, baby and mother reached the green wooden seat, and came to rest. The baby slept soundly with the soother touching her velvet pink cheeks, hand on pillow, a picture of purity. The woman heard a coughing noise coming from the nearby gun turret, and managed to see the tip of a rifle and a face peering out from the darkness. Smells of cabbage and burnt potatoes wafted over from behind the slanting sheets of protective steel.

'Is that your baby?' an English voice called out. She could barely see the face belonging to the voice. She replied yes, and smiled. The situation reminded her of the confessional. Dark and supposedly anonymous, 'Is that you, my child?' She knew the priest personally. Did he identify her sins with his 'Good morning, Mary', and think to himself, 'and I know what you were up to last night!' She blushed at the secrets given away through the ceremony. Yes, she nervously answered again, it was her baby, a little girl. First-time mothers rarely resist the temptation to talk about their offspring. Forgetting her initial shyness, she told the voice of when the baby was born, the early problems of all-night crying, now teething, how she could crawl backwards and gurgle. In fact all the minutiae that unite mothers everywhere.

The voice responded. It too had a son, a few months older than her child, away in Germany at the army base at Münster. The voice too talked with the quiet affection that binds fathers everywhere to their children. The English voice talked out from the turret as if addressing the darkening lines of silhouettes in the distance beyond the park. Factory pipes, chimney tops, church spires, domes all listened impassively to the Englishman's declaration of paternal love. The scene was strange, for although Belfast's sterile geography slipped into classical forms with dusk and heavy rain-clouds, the voice and the woman knew the folly of such innocent communication. They politely finished their conversation, said goodbye and the woman pushed her pram homewards. The voice remained in the turret, watchful and anxious. Home she went, past vanloads of workers leering out past the uneasy presence of foot patrols, past the Church.

'Let us give each other the sign of peace' they said at Mass. The only sign Belfast knew was two fingers pointing towards Heaven. Life was self-contained, the couple often declared, just like flats. No need to go outside.

She did go outside, however. Over the weeks the voice had become a name, John. It had become a friend, someone to listen to, to talk to. No face, but a person removed from the city's grotesqueries and colourlessness. She sat on the bench, the pram in front, the baby asleep, listening, talking, looking ahead at the hospital corridors stretching languidly before her. He talked of his wife, and the city he came from. In some ways, remote as another planet, in others as familiar as the earth itself. Memories of childhood aspirations grown out of back-to-back slum, of disappointment, the pain of failure, the fear of rejection in adolescence. Visions of Germany, Teutonic efficiency and emotional hardness; Malta and Cyprus, exotic, crimson, romantic, legendary, the holiday brochures come to life.

She told him of her family, of escaping through books, longing to endure noble pain and mysterious wildness, to experience outrageous immorality, to be as aloof as Yeats himself. To be memorable, she told him, was her awful imagination-consuming desire, even if only to have her name on a wall that would stand for centuries. She told him of Donegal, its vitality and freshness, its windswept, heather-blown beauty, savage waves plummeting and spume crashing onto sheer cliffs and jagged rocks. She tried to paint a picture of the place and tell how forlorn and vulnerable it made her feel, but her expressions were inadequate, her words mere clichés. She felt she had begun to talk in slogans.

Each week the voice and the woman learned more of each other. No physical contact was needed, no face-to-face encounter to judge reaction, no touching to confirm amity, no threat of dangerous intimacy. It was a meeting of minds, as she explained later to her husband, a new opinion, a common bond, an opening of vistas. He disclosed his ambitions to become a pilot, to watch the land, fields and horizons spread out beneath him — a patchwork quilt of dappled colours and textures. She wanted to be remembered by writing on walls. And all this time the city's skyline and distant buildings watched and listened.

It was April now. More slogans had appeared, white and dripping, on the city walls. 'Brits out. Peace in.' A simple equation for the writer. 'Loose talk claims lives', another shouted menacingly. The messages, the woman decided, had acquired a more ominous tone. The baby had grown and could sit up without support. New political solutions had been pro-posed and rejected, interparamilitary feuding had broken out and subsided, four soldiers and two policemen had been blown to smithereens in separate incidents, and a building a day had been bombed by the Provos. It had been a fairly normal month by Belfast's standards. The level of violence was no more or less acceptable than at other times. Life has to continue, after all.

One day — it was, perhaps, the last day in April — her husband returned home panting and trembling a little. He asked if she had been to the park, and she replied that she had. Taking her by the hand, he led her to the wall on the left of their driveway. She felt her heart sink and thud. She

6

felt her face redden. Her mouth was suddenly dry. She could not speak. In huge angry letters the message spat itself out,

TOUT

The four-letter word covered the whole wall. It clanged in her brain, its venom rushed through her body. Suspicion was enough to condemn. What creature had skulked to paint the word? Whose arm, dismembered and independent, had swung from tin to wall to deliver judgement? The job itself was not well done, she had seen better. The letters were uneven, paint splattered down from the crossed T, the U looked a misshapen O. The workmanship was poor, the impact perfect.

Her husband led her back into the kitchen. The baby was crying loudly but the woman did not seem to hear. Like sleep-walkers, they sat down on the settee. The woman began to sob. Her shoulders heaved in bursts as she gasped hysterically. Her husband took her in his arms gently and tried to make her sorrow his. Already he shared her fear.

'What did you talk about? Did you not realise how dangerous it was? We must leave.' He spoke quickly, making plans. Selling the house and car, finding a job in London or Dublin, far away from Belfast; mortgages, removals, savings, the tawdry affairs of normal living stunned her, making her more confused.

'I told him nothing', she sobbed, 'what could I tell? We talked about life, everything, but not about here.' She trembled, trying to control herself.

'We just chatted about reading walls, families, anything at all. Oh Seán, it was as innocent as that. A meeting of minds we called it, for it was little else.'

She looked into her husband's face and saw he did not fully understand. There was a hint of jealousy, of resentment at not being part of their communion. Her hands fell on her lap, resting in resignation. What was the point of explanation? She lifted her baby from the floor. Pressing the tiny face and body

7

to her breast, she felt all her hopes and desires for a better life become one with the child's struggle for freedom. How could she invite the trauma of war into this new pure soul? Belfast and innocence. The two seemed incongruous and yet it must be done. The child's hands wandered over her face, their eyes met. At once that moment of maternal and filial love eclipsed her fear, gave her the impetus to escape.

For nine months she had been unable to accept the reality of her condition. Absurd, for the massive bump daily shifted position and thumped against her. When her daughter was born, she had been overwhelmed by love for her and amazed at her own ability to give life. By nature she was a dreamy person, given to moments of fancy. She played out historical, romantic, literary roles in her imagination. She wondered at her competence in fulfilling the role of mother. Could it be measured? This time she knew it could. She really did not care if they maimed her or even murdered her. She did care about her daughter. She was her touchstone, her anchor to virtue. Not for her child a legacy of fear, revulsion or hatred. With the few hours respite the painters had left between judgement and sentence she determined to leave Belfast's walls behind.

The next few nights were spent in troubled, restless, sleep. The message remained on the wall outside. The neighbours pretended not to notice and the matter was not discussed. She and the baby remained indoors despite the refreshing May breezes and blue skies. Her husband had given in his notice at the office, for health reasons, he suggested to his colleagues. An aunt had been contacted in Dublin. The couple did not answer knocks at the door, carefully examined the shape and size of mail delivered and always paused when they answered the telephone. Espionage and treachery were the order of the day, or so it seemed. It was time for reappraisal, for scrutiny of goals in life and the opportunity for survival. They agreed they had to escape for their lives were at risk now. Touting is punishable by death, tradition has ordained it so. The cause and its victory must be pursued.

Their cases and tea-chests were packed in the hallway. Old wedding gifts, still unused, library books hopelessly out-of-date, maternity clothes and sports wear, chipped ornaments and cutlery. They cluttered up the place as they awaited the day of departure. An agent was taking care of selling the house and getting a suitable price. A job was promised with an insurance company in Dublin, and their aunt had prepared a room for them. They told no one in the street. They would write later (omitting the address, naturally), enclosing a cheque for milk and bread bills. Every eventuality was covered, every potential loop-hole filled. Their exodus, their little conspiracy, was planned with exactitude and cunning. Then they waited for the night they were to leave home.

The mini-van was to call at eleven on Monday night, when it would be dark enough to park and pack their belongings and themselves without too much suspicion being aroused. The firm had been very understanding when the nature of their work had been explained; there was no conflict of loyalties involved in the exercise. They agreed to drive them to Dublin at extra cost, changing drivers at Newry on the way down.

Monday finally arrived. The couple nervously laughed about how smoothly everything had gone. Privately, they each expected something to go wrong. The baby was fed, and played with, the radio listened to and the clock watched. The hours dragged by as the couple waited for eleven to chime.

She wondered what had happened to the voice, John. Had he missed her visits? Was he safe? Quickly she dismissed him from her thoughts. It was her selfishness and silly notions that had got them into this mess. She never had a great store of moral courage, content to lie down and accept in true Croppy fashion, as her husband always said. She had never been outstanding or bold, having gone along as peacefully as possible. It was her child who had given her strength, life and freedom from her old self. But would they make it?

They listened to the news at nine. Huddled together in their anxiety, they kept vigil in the darkening room. Rain had begun to pour from black thunder clouds. Everywhere it was quiet and still. Hushed and cold they waited. Ten o'clock, and it was now dark. A blustery wind had risen making the lattice separation next door bang and clatter. At ten to eleven, her husband went into the sittingroom to watch for the mini-van. His footsteps clamped noisily on the floorboards as he paced back and forth. The baby slept.

A black shape glided slowly up the street and backed into the driveway. It was eleven. The van had arrived. Her husband asked to see identification and then they began to load up the couple's belongings. Settee, chairs, television, washing machine — all were dumped hastily, it was no time to worry about breakages. She stood holding the sleeping baby in the livingroom as the men worked anxiously between van and house. The scene was so unreal, the circumstances absolutely incredible, she thought 'What have I done?' Recollections of her naivety, her insensitivity to historical fact and political climate were stupefying. She had seen women who had been tarred and feathered, heard of people who had been shot in the head, boys who had been knee-capped, all for suspected fraternising with troops. The catalogue of violence spilled out before her as she realised the gravity and possible repercussions of her alleged misdemeanour.

A voice called her, 'Mary, come on now. We have to go. Don't worry, we're all together.' Her husband led her to the locked and waiting van. Handing the baby to him, she climbed up beside the driver, took the baby as her husband sat down beside her and waited for the engine to start. The van slowly manoeuvered out onto the street and down the main road. They felt more cheerful now, a little like refugees seeking safety and freedom not too far away. As they approached the motorway bridge, two figures with something clutched in their hands stood side by side in the darkness. She closed her eyes tightly, expecting bursts of gunfire. The van shot past. Relieved, she asked her husband what they were doing at this time of night.

'Writing slogans on the wall' he replied.

The furtiveness of the painters seemed ludicrous and petty as she recalled the heroic and literary characteristics with which she had endowed them. What did they matter? The travellers sat in silence as the van sped past the city suburbs, the glare of police and army barracks, on out and further out into the countryside. Past sleeping villages and silent fields, past white-washed farmhouses and barking dogs. On to Newry where they said goodbye to their driver as the new one stepped in. Far along the coast with Rostrevor's twinkling lights opposite the bay, down to the Border check and a drowsy soldier waving them through. Out of the North, safe, relieved and heading for Dublin.

She noticed, as the van drove along the Liffey quay that wall messages existed here too. Their meanness saddened her. Wall-reading had been fun, a spur for the imagination, a way to be remembered. All her life she had longed to be remembered through walls, the people's medium. Now the medium itself was as destructive, as deadening as the concrete it was written on. She had neither the strength of character nor the fine moral fibre necessary to be remembered. Yet, strangely, despite disappointment, she felt glad in a peculiar way and not such an abysmal failure after all. One person, the voice John at least, would deliver her memory to his family and friends, would perhaps pray for her ambitions and maybe even admire her simple-minded ignorance of Belfast's sordid heart.

Some days later in Belfast the neighbours discovered the house vacant, the people next door received a letter and a cheque from Dublin. Remarks about the peculiar couple were made over hedges and cups of coffee. The message on the wall was painted over by the couple who had bought the house when it went up for sale. They too were ordinary people, living a self-contained life, worrying over finance and babies, promotion and local gossip. He too had an office job, but his wife was merely a housekeeper for him. She was

11

sensible, down to earth, and not in the least inclined to wall-reading.

the fourth scenic route

Soinbhe Lally

Strips of chrome on the car bonnet deflected the fiery glow of sunset and threw light into George's eyes.

'Bugger,' he muttered as the tyres crunched on the gravel edge. He peered at the road ahead. It curved sharply round a jutting piece of rock.

'Bugger,' he said again when he felt a tug on his steering wheel.

Myrtle winced. She disliked coarse language. Unfastening her seat-belt she eased her aching back while George carefully slowed down, allowing for the weight of their small touring caravan behind. He drew into a lay-by which was carved out of a rocky mountain wall.

Myrtle removed her glasses. They had dark lenses clipped over them. She used a pink tissue to wipe perspiration from her small puckered eyes. When George stood in front of the car swearing at the punctured tyre she pursed her mouth, making it small and puckered too.

'Don't miss Donegal,' he mimicked in a high pitched voice, 'the coast is superb.' He glared at the rugged wall above and the crooked, sparsely covered fields below. 'I don't know what

Marjorie saw in this place. This is the fourth scenic route we've done today and not a bit of decent land to be seen.' He strode to the rear of the car and flung open the boot.

'Well, I think Marjorie should know,' Myrtle argued, 'she tours a great deal.' She stepped from the car, crossed the road and sat on the low wall which protected motorists from the steep incline below. Drawing her cardigan around her shoulders she examined the view. On the slopes she saw woolly sheep, fluffy yellow charolais calves, tough wiry grass standing in tufts and, far below, a small white beach and a field with caravans.

Day was slipping away. On the darkening sea there remained only a red afterglow of sunset. Myrtle craned her neck to see if there were lavatories.

'Look George,' she called, 'there's a site down there. If you're going to take much longer we could stop there.'

George snorted in reply and levered the jack furiously. His thick neck bulged and his cheeks swelled.

'There's a building of some sort. I can't quite see but it must be toilets. Marjorie says small sites are the best.'

'Marjorie says, Marjorie says,' George mimicked sarcastically. Nevertheless when he drove down the steeply winding road to the foot of the mountain and arrived at the green field with caravans he drove in there instead of going on to a bigger site in the town some miles beyond.

They chose a sheltered nook to the lee side of a larger caravan. George reversed in and Myrtle waved signals to him when he came too close to a tent pitched on the other side.

She noted with disapproval that the site building consisted of only a single lavatory with a tap on the outside wall. It was impossible to wash in the caravan. George had no sense of privacy. She needed to wash properly. She had felt sticky all day. The last site had showers and a launderette, television and pool rooms. She had expected to have a proper wash there, and rolling her toilet things in a towel went to the shower room.

She heard a distinctly masculine grunt from one of the cubicles.

'These are the ladies' showers,' she said, boldly confronting the drawn curtain. A girl tittered and Myrtle, appalled, realised there were two of them in there.

George should complain.

'More power to them,' he said and he laughed so Myrtle never got her shower.

They had already had tea in a picnic area near Seafield. Now there was only coffee to be made and a bed made up. Myrtle preferred sheets. Sleeping bags, she felt, were improper. The way they zipped together made her think of the promiscuous young people who squatted in tents all over camp sites. It made one wonder what on earth their parents were thinking of. Even here, in the tent beside them there were two young people dressed alike in denim and zip fasteners. They certainly didn't look married.

She smoothed the sheets and fluffed the pillows. They were white and clean, except where George's hair oil stained them. He liked his hair combed back in slick waves. The hair oil held it that way but it made nasty stains on the pillow slips.

The gas light threw a cosy glow around the interior of the caravan. Myrtle loved the caravan. Everything was so compact, so neat. There wasn't even room for George to be untidy. He kept his fishing tackle in the boot of the car.

Someone knocked on the door. George opened it.

'Can I come in?' a voice asked. A man, browned and bent by weather and age climbed in and sat on the edge of a flowered cushion. 'I'm James Hegarty,' he introduced himself. 'The field is mine. One pound a night I charge.'

Myrtle took a pound from her handbag and handed it to George.

'We'll only stop one night. We're touring,' he explained. James accepted the note and rose to go.

15

'A nice quiet place here,' he said. 'That's an artist there, and his wife.' He pointed towards the large caravan beside. 'It's hard to beat round here for scenery.'

'Now, I wouldn't agree with you at all about that,' George objected, 'have you ever been to County Down?'

'I haven't,' James replied.

'Well the land there is all soft and green and there's nice round hills. I've never seen the like of it.'

'Is that so?'

'We were down that way last year. Lovely, it was. Isn't that right, Myrtle?'

Myrtle agreed.

'I'd like to see that,' James said. 'Of course there's some good land in this county too, down by Letterkenny, but out here is where the tourists come.'

Myrtle felt it was time to interrupt.

'Goodnight, Mr. Hegarty,' she said. If he stayed much longer he would expect a cup of tea.

'Goodnight ma'am,' James said.

'Goodnight,' George echoed.

'Goodnight to you too, sir,' James said and he touched his cap.

George turned down the gas. The light extinguished itself with a pop. He climbed over the small mound Myrtle made in the bed and settled himself down, breathing noisily. His arm brushed the lace frill of her nightgown. He placed a hand on her shoulder.

'What is it George?' She flinched from his touch.

'Nothing.' He rolled over to face the wall. 'I might fish a bit tomorrow. Some likely looking rocks about.'

Myrtle was pleased. She would be able to wash while he was out.

'Do put your shirt on dear,' she pressed him when he left the caravan before breakfast wearing only his pants, and a

16

towel draped around his neck. Myrtle didn't like seeing his hairy chest and morning bristle on his chin. It was improper she felt, exposing his manhood in the daylight.

'Stuff it,' George said coarsely and Myrtle hoped the young couple from the tent hadn't overheard. They were sitting on the grass in front of their tent eating cornflakes. Their kettle was steaming over a butane stove. They smiled at her. She nodded and abruptly retreated into the caravan.

They were quite unashamed nowadays. They didn't even try to pretend.

She prepared breakfast, pausing a moment to look at some cows which wandered on to the beach and waded into the shallow waves near the edge of the sand. Sun beamed through the morning haze and already the air was warm.

Over boiled eggs they watched the progress of the cows. They were now belly deep in the sea.

'It probably cools them off,' George suggested.

'I don't think it is very hygienic,' Myrtle said. 'They probably do... things out there. It shouldn't be allowed.'

'Aw, you're always trying to make rules.'

'And you're always trying to get around them.'

George changed the subject. 'I'll fish till about four.'

'What about lunch?'

'I'll have it when I come in.'

'At four?'

'Is there any reason why I can't have lunch at four?'

'Marjorie says Tom always brings sandwiches and a flask when he goes fishing.'

'Marjorie says! Well I'm not lugging a portable cafeteria across the rocks with me. I'll have my lunch at four. Then we'll pack up and move on.'

Myrtle gazed past him, across his shoulder. 'I suppose she bleaches it,' she said.

'What?' George turned to follow her gaze.

'Don't look now. They'll see you. It's her, she must be the artist's wife.'

17

In the neighbouring caravan the artist and his wife were sitting down to breakfast. He was silvery-haired and distinguished looking Myrtle conceded. His wife's back was to them and only her unnaturally blonde hair could be seen.

'Mmm,' George grunted and turned back.

When he went out Myrtle wiped the table and folded it away, washed dishes, put cups and plates in their little compartments and swept up crumbs. She rinsed the tea-towel and hung it on a string which she tied between the caravan and the car rack. The young man from the tent passed coming from the refuse tip and she felt obliged to return his friendly good morning. Then she drew the caravan curtains, locked both halves of the door and filled the basin she used for washing herself.

She carried several plastic basins on tour, one for washing dishes, one for personal washing and other smaller basins for lesser chores.

She undressed her upper half and sponged it. Then she soaped her armpits and used a small pink ladies' razor. She finished up with talcum, then dressed the upper half, undressed the lower half and repeated the routine. This took longer because there was more to shave.

Marjorie didn't shave hers but Myrtle thought it more hygienic. Her buzz, Marjorie called it. She sent them a card when she and Tom took a second honeymoon for their silver anniversary. Greetings from Buzzerville, she wrote, wish you were here. It wasn't very nice. Of course it made George laugh a lot.

She finished with more talcum, taking care not to sprinkle it on the patch of carpet that covered the floor of the caravan. Then she dressed and drew back the curtains.

Yonder was George on his rock. White surf splashed gently below his feet. Only his profile could be distinguished among the jagged promontories. It was a good profile. Stocky, and rounded a little at the middle. Viewed from here he might be anybody, an angling journalist, a TV weatherman, a politician

18

holidaying incognito. George did all right, of course, as a weigh-bridge clerk. But working with lorry drivers all day wasn't very improving for him.

Myrtle carried to the beach a magazine, a folding chair, a sunhat, her glasses with sun lenses clipped on and a cardigan. She glanced disapprovingly at the young people from the tent. They shared a rug further along the beach and were smearing sun lotion on one another. Myrtle read her magazine. The artist and his wife walked past in knee-length shorts and bare feet. Each carried a bag. Myrtle nodded and smiled but they didn't notice and padded on across the sand.

At half past three she prepared lunch, lettuce, tomatoes and ham which she stored in matching plastic containers in the small gas fridge. She put the kettle on the stove and set the table. The kettle whistled and she looked to see if George was coming. Yes, there he was, no longer fishing. He had moved back along the rock. There were other people there too. Perhaps he was chatting. She waited a while. Then she stood in front of the caravan and waved.

'George!' George waved back. He waved his fishing rod and then waved his satchel. He must have caught something. She returned to the caravan and went on waiting. She lit the gas and put the kettle back to boil.

'George,' she called once again from the front of the caravan. She cupped her hands around her mouth. 'Tea's ready!' He waved again. He had climbed back up the rock and was sitting there with the other people. It was the artist and his wife. Myrtle could see her bleached hair.

'George,' she shouted. The couple from the tent must have noticed the irritation in her voice. The young man approached her.

'I think the tide has come in,' he said.

'Yes,' Myrtle agreed distantly, 'my husband always stops fishing when the tide comes in. I was just letting him know lunch... tea is ready.' She corrected herself. She did not want him to know they were having lunch at five o'clock.

'I think the tide comes right around those rocks,' he explained. 'They were nearly covered yesterday.'

'You mean he can't get in?' She looked again at George and realized he was swinging his bag and waving his rod because he needed help. Her breath caught in her throat. 'What will I do?'

The young man looked uneasily towards the caravan. The kettle was whistling shrilly. 'I think you had better take off that kettle,' he murmured helpfully.

Myrtle darted inside.

'What will I do?' she repeated when she came out again.

'I'll look for a rope,' the young man offered. He glanced about vaguely at the cliffs and then at the mountain behind. Its steep side was speckled with white backs of grazing sheep. 'I'll try up the road,' he said and hurried off.

Myrtle ran to the water's edge to shout to George. The rising tide forced her to retreat several yards up the beach before the man from the tent arrived with James and a length of rope.

'Are they in danger?' Myrtle asked James.

'Well, now,' he equivocated, 'if the moon was full them rocks would cover right over.'

The young man undressed and tied the rope around his waist. The girl from the tent stood a little apart watching him. James inspected the knot.

'A knot like that will never hold,' he said. He untied it and took several minutes to tie in its place a bulky intricate knot. The young man turned towards the water. 'Wait now,' said James, 'there's splices on this rope.' He searched the full length of the rope for old splices, examined them carefully, tested them by pulling them between his gnarled fists and finally satisfied himself that the rope would hold. 'Bear to the right,' he cautioned, 'bear to the right for the current on the left would carry you off altogether.'

'I think I can cope,' the young man assured him. He was lithe and brown, and looked fit for heroic action.

'Isn't he brave,' Myrtle quavered, 'to go swimming right out there.'

'My husband is a strong swimmer,' the girl reassured her.

'Your husband,' Myrtle echoed and seized with a sense of comradeship she clutched the girl by her denim sleeve. It was cute, really, for the two of them to dress alike. Like twins, she thought.

The rope sank in the water and trailed in the wet sand. The young man pulled himself back in on it. 'Hold it up,' he said, 'pass it out over your heads like this.' He demonstrated. Old James stood on the dry sand holding the end of the rope. The girl stood ankle deep in the water with her jeans rolled up to her knees. She passed the rope over her head to Myrtle who stood further out in the water, shying from the waves that splashed her underclothes and made her skirt stick to her thighs.

The rope was too short. The young man pulled himself back in, wheezing and snorting and stood shaking the water out of his hair.

'It might be handier to let them wait there another while till the tide goes out' James suggested.

'But won't the sea come right over them?'

'Well it all depends on the moon.' James calculated painstakingly. 'The new moon was Thursday a week ago so there won't be a top tide for another four days. I doubt them rocks won't cover this tide. Anyway,' he added looking at the frothy track of the waves on the sand, 'I think maybe the tide's going out now.'

Myrtle glared at George on his rock. He waved cheerfully. He was eating sandwiches now and drinking a cup of something from the artist's thermos flask. He didn't even realise how much anxiety he had caused her, and he had made her get her clothes all wet into the bargain.

It was over an hour before George got in. Myrtle watched indignantly from the caravan as he waded to the shore with his fishing gear and then waded back out again to help the artist and his wife with their bags. The three walked together across the beach. They stopped at the tent to exchange noisy greetings with the young couple. George delved in his satchel and gave them two small flounder. Myrtle went out and joined them. She hadn't really thanked the young people properly.

'I've been out of my mind with worry,' she greeted George, 'we thought you would be drowned.'

'This is Simon Magee,' George interrupted, 'and Jennifer.'

'We're Babs and Mike,' said one of the young couple.

They shook hands. Then the kettle whistled.

'Just what we need, a cup of tea,' George said and he invited them all inside. Myrtle wondered would there be enough salad to go round.

The artist went to his caravan and came back with whiskey. 'Here's what'll warm us up,' he said and poured it into the cups of tea.

'Just a teeny drop,' Myrtle protested and she added more sugar to sweeten it.

James dropped by to see if they were staying another night. He collected his pound and accepted a cup of tea with his whiskey. George unearthed some bottles of beer from the bottom of the wardrobe and offered them around.

'Here's a man,' James addressed the artist, 'who thinks you should do your painting in County Down.'

'Now that's what I'd call scenery,' added George. 'It's the best land I've ever seen. And well cared for too.'

'Well naturally,' the artist explained, 'that sort of scenery might seem more beautiful to a practical man like yourself, or from a farmer's point of view. But around here is the sort of landscape that interests an artist.' He waved towards the mountain.

'But there's not even grass growing up there,' George argued looking up at the stony rubble on the slopes.

'That's the whole point,' said the artist. 'An artist can give that significance. Meaning. Look, there's a sunset now. Lots of colour, light and all that, but I look at that, and I say, what does that mean.'

Myrtle rinsed the cups and saucers. She insisted on the other women remaining seated. There was only room for one person to work in a caravan.

'What does that mean?' the artist repeated emphatically.

George gazed at the sunset and its golden glory reflected in his features gave his expression a visionary glow. 'I'd say it means rain,' he said.

'That's right,' James agreed.

They were late going to bed. The excitement of the evening lingered even after everyone had left. They undressed and Myrtle shed a scent of talcum around the enclosed space as she took off her clothes. George climbed into bed beside her.

'Who smells so nice?' He nuzzled her neck and his rough chin rasped against her skin.

'Stop it George,' she squealed.

'Oh come on.' He groped clumsily as she squirmed from him. Then he drew back abruptly.

'Bugger,' he groaned, 'bald again'. He rolled over to his own side of the bed.

•

the funeral

Maureen O'Connor

She'd have been happy to know they buried her here, near
the sea, so she would. That was the daughter's doing, tho' the
eldest son felt it not right with her parents above in a family
grave in Glasnevin and plenty of space there for her. Her
father, years ago, made sure of that, not trusting the son-in-
law to see to the practical side of things at all.

He was a great old man, her father, they tell me. A city
man, born and bred, and gone long before she came first to
the West and never rested 'til she owned her own bit of boggy
land on this side of the hill, with the lake before it and hills
beyond that again. And what did she do then but get a local
builder to build her a shoe-box of a house, full of big windows
and white walls, with a wooden stair mounting up to the attic.

Do you remember the time when there was no bohereen
at all to the house? The height of foolishness. They had to
lug the shopping and things up the hill, round the rocks in
wet grass and everyone expected to like it. Getting the turf
and the gas up was the worst, so it was. It was Bartley said it
to her.

'You lay the road down first and then build the house.'

24

She didn't listen to him then but later she owned it was right. It should have been done the first day. A relief to see the JCB in, after the first year, carving the width of a car across the garrai and laying down the stones and gravel. She came often the first and second year it was finished, and oftener again as she grew older.

Himself had one leg in Kerry all the time tho' he seemed happy enough spending summers here. A great man to walk; think nothing of seven or eight miles in all weather, and some of that down by the shore. We heard he had himself cremated and the ashes scattered near his mother's grave in a Kerry churchyard. They were nice enough and gay enough in their times here so it is queer to be thinking all the time of death and burying.

The long grass here should be scythed. The place is packed out anyway and a new one promised this long time. Half the grave-stones are flattened, but hers is so small and low that it will be covered with sand and nettles in no time. A friend of hers from Dublin that brought it in the back of his car, a piece of a granite rock and only a rough cross scratched on it. You'd think they could do better than that, probably the daughter again. The son told me there was a fine Celtic Cross above in Glasnevin such as not many bother ordering these days.

Maybe she found the house too lonely after Himself died. Tho' she came often on her own and you could see her planting bushes and trees around the garrai and painting the windows. She had pictures on the walls inside too that she did herself sometime. Queer, big ones, all of rocks and bits of sea. Above in the attic she had what she called her 'studio', tho' all I ever could make of it was an empty space with more white walls, and an old wooden table you'd throw out it was that worn.

She was nice enough in her way but always going to the shore, whatever the weather. They used to see her in all seasons walking away down the bohereen and getting lost among the rocks. Sometimes she'd be sketching, more times she'd be doing nothing at all, and then she took a great interest in those high pools where the cuan mara grow. Wanted to know about them, she did. She even cut one off the rock and ate it one day but was sorry after. I don't know was it she was sick after it or sorry she killed it. She was funny that way. Scared of a bat and wouldn't kill it if one got into the house.

The family are saying it was an accident. The priest is giving her the benefit of the doubt but I dunno. What in God's name was she doing out there at the back of the rock in a high wind and she not too good on the legs? There's nothing to see but the sea and Clare and maybe the Islands. She could have seen all that from the strand so what was she doing above on the rock? Someone told me she was a divil for drawing birds and looking at the colours in the waves. Maybe she got dizzy or went too near the edge and the feet went from under her. A sad way to go even if she was a bit strange.

The younger daughter isn't shedding a tear. She's as calm as you please, looking away off to sea as if she thought her mother was swimming away out there and not here beside us in the shallow grave. Dublin people are all queer. You'd never know them. You think you do, and then they do something like this; slipping into the tide, God help us, and being buried among us.

They're putting a tin plate above on a rock in her place, giving her name and RIP after it. It wasn't as if she was one of us like the O'Flahertys, they have the same down there at the harbour below the house. She used walk down the hill, say a prayer at the rock tho' she never knew the Flahertys on the piece of tin stuck there on the rock.

It is as if she didn't know where she belonged, here or above in the city. Brid visited her there once and it was as different from her cottage here as you could imagine. All modern and nice. A proper garden and flower-beds. Carpet on the floors and brass shining on the door. She'd have none of that here.

The garrai was never dug. She planted trees and bushes all

right but they're the same we all have; fuschia and escalonia and a mountain ash at the gable end of the house. She was a nuisance too with her weeds. She'd let the purple strife wild round the place and the geosadan thick in the grass. And the walls were never improved, she wouldn't part with the loose stone and hated the concrete. You'd see her in late summer, scraping the rocks, and if you asked, she'd talk about dyeing wool with the crotal and all class of foolishness. But she was happy in herself. Never minded the weather. She had the same old anorak and boots as long as I knew her.

And the cat. What'll happen to the cat? Up and down, all that distance, in a basket made specially for it as if it was a prize cat. Maybe one of the daughters will take the cat.

Will they sell up the place now or keep it? It would fetch a good price; it was well built and she looked after it if it wasn't all that comfortable itself. No central-heating like new houses and no 'phone. A local wouldn't need a 'phone, only the new lot working at the TV or someone out of the factories.

They're finished the prayers, all in Irish. Wasn't her Irish terrible? And she'd talk it and talk it. Sure she tried anyway. There's a lot here can't answer the priest in Irish; came down from Dublin, a lot of them. Himself was well known so that's why so many turned up. And the family. They used be here on holidays when they were children, renting a house for the summer. Queer to see them, men and women. Children of their own now.

We're finished at last, Thank God: the wind has me frozen. God rest her anyway whatever happened.

She'd have wanted us to go back for something hot to warm the cold out of us.

The family might know that.

We'll see if they hurry off in cars or wait around a bit.

You don't want to be pushing in at a time like this.

Or keeping out either

A body wouldn't know what to do.

27

gala night

Hilda Murphy

'Never do anything you don't really want to do,' said my tutor. 'You're a generous young woman, Miss Furlong, but your kindness needs to be disciplined.' At twenty, one is more interested in upstaging counsellors than listening to them, and with an assurance that I would go out of my way to be as nasty as possible I left, clutching my latest, commendable examination results. Everyone seemed to think I was kind. This was not the case. It was just part of the good fortune I seemed to possess in embarrassing superabundance. The good looks were my father's and the brain my mother's, and while I could see that the opposite would have been disastrous, it was my own humility which made me wonder if one would not have been enough. From my parents, too, I had lots of lovely money. They had even died when I was sixteen, for what, after all, does one want with parents after that?

It's all so easy, I though, as Dublin's Renoir light cleared a way through the mist above slender houses from which I had not only aesthetic pleasure but substantial ground rents. Why did everyone think I was kind? It was easy to give; receiving would have killed me. The flat on my own was too opulent. Next week heavy Louisa and selfish Helen would be back to provide human irritation. Meanwhile, my home must accommodate the lame and the lonely, the overflow from my brother's outrageously successful medical practice. Mortimer kept open house for his patients; always ensuring that the house was open enough to allow for his own escape. I was the understudy. I knew exactly who was expected. I also knew who was not, for the theatre, the judiciary, the academics, the newspapers, and the less rustic representatives of government and Church would be at a far from private Private View. My charges were only going to meet each other. Mortimer, for all his compassion, had never realised that lonely people don't want to meet other lonely people.

As always, the least welcome were the first to arrive, and I noticed Trevor, the elderly prima gravida. I always thought of him thus — it was Mortimer's absent-minded comment when Trevor was doing a Ph.D. So fully and naively did I follow the doctrine of being nice to the unfortunates that it scarcely occurred to me that he might not see himself as a Black Baby. He had, after all, late in life, secured a university teaching post (he would have put it in that solemn, letter-of-application type of language). And if he hadn't made it in Dublin, in spite of much hanging around the relevant department and being mistaken for the Dean's manservant, he also had a job in America, where he was called professor. Who would not go to great lengths, even cross the Atlantic, for such thrills? He had dressed up tonight, in a new Burton's suit, slightly ill-fitting. He looked quite spruce. I must think of something to ask him about the PhD, I thought, as he appeared in the kitchen.

'You're looking very nice, Ruth,' he said. I felt he had probably rehearsed something more daring on his way down the stairs but then couldn't quite manage it.

'That party frock suits you.'

Party frock? The kilt and T-shirt I was wearing were un-related to either parties or frocks. I made some suitably in-

29

coherent reply. Poor Trevor. So much dandruff; so little hair. The wave of pity I felt for him was so live with the contrast between my assets and his drabness that it was probably not sympathy at all, I thought wildly, but vanity.

Trevor had taken a box of corn plasters from his pocket and was sliding it up and down between his thumb and second finger.

'I know you're mad about music,' he went on.

Incorrect. In fact I am tone deaf. Once, again on Mortimer's behalf, I had attended a recital in the hope of encouraging a patient who was trying to substitute oratorio for hypochondria. Trevor had turned up beside me, having presumably been given the other free ticket. He seemed to have remembered every word of our insignificant conversation. He had the good memory of one who was so self-conscious as to be unable to forget anything, and whose life was so empty that the merest greeting was an event. Trevor was very proud of his memory, as people are invariably proud of their least attractive characteristics. Some conventional expression of interest was used to involve me.

'Would you like to come to the Opera next week?'

It was the slight shake in his voice that disarmed me. I thanked him, agreed, and escaped to the sittingroom. How I wished he had invited one of the other girls – Maeve, the eternal student who, at thirty eight, still carried a book at parties and thought she was Ireland's answer to Simone de Beauvoir. Or Celine, who had left the convent on some abstruse theological principle and whose pretty faced looked unfinished without the strengthening wimple, listening with party expressions to Trevor's transport arrangement for our outing. Operation Get-from-Harcourt-Street-to-the-Gaiety did not seem to me a major one, but how wrong I was.

Came Gala Night and we drove the few yards to the theatre and then returned almost to my halldoor to park. Trevor was greatly preoccupied with the gallant duty of keeping me on the inside of the pavement. He was also very conscientious about grasping my elbow at the kerb and even not at the kerb, and he only let go to disappear into the public lavatory at the side of Stephen's Green. I walked on very slowly, realising that Trevor was not quite normal. However, a sense of high-mindedness, of vocation, sustained me throughout the charade of a glamorous evening. Trevor had certain formulae. I noticed, certain customs of a festive nature that were inclined to get confused, like buying me flowers (woman) and ice-cream (child). He even rather disconcertingly, took a photo-graph of me during the interval. However, amidst the trivia of the occasion, it was unlikely that anyone noticed. The Dress Circle was not (as it were) my galere, and the Brown Thomas matrons, the middle-aged brides of ambitious barristers, the artificially double-barrelled names were just extras in Trevor's party. I was glad to be able to lay them on, and I introduced him, stressing the doctoral title.

Having no interest in music, I could find little to occupy my thoughts between the pleasant tune in the first act and the same tune (I think) repeated in the last. I wondered how much longer it could go on. The alert bearing — and he appeared to be quite awake — of the military gentleman in attendance on the President was impressive. Because he didn't take out his gun, and actually *shoot* the soprano, it made me wonder if this was perhaps Colonel Drew, the Protestant, who so unfailingly, daily, it seemed, represented the Great Man at St. Patrick's Cathedral. I had only my thoughts to entertain me, so they were wild indeed. By now, Trevor was holding my hand; another of his taking-a-girl-out gestures, I supposed, and thought no more of it. In any case, I was just about unconscious with boredom.

The feeling of anaesthesia fortunately persisted throughout dinner. There was much tasting of the wine, and instruction, of which the waiter made no note, about how the steaks were to be done. 'Twere well 'twere done quickly would have been my only wish, had I been truthful. I asked Trevor about America, and he told me. He started at Cobh. It was a jumble of sneakers and vacations and tuxedos and campuses and credits that I did not bother to follow. Trevor seemed confident that he was selling it to me successfully, and mentioned places I must see and people he would introduce to me. I was, in fact, going there the following year (Mortimer, God forgive him, must have let this slip) so I agreed to all the proposed expeditions, knowing that America would at least be bigger than Dublin and that another evening like this need not take place. When Trevor had finished his cigar, I felt we could safely ring down the curtain. Even my vocabulary was getting theatrical. Not yet. There was another rule from the social game.

'Come and see mother. She's expecting you.'

When it became clear that any postponement of this would mean the sacrifice of another evening, I agreed. Trevor took my ungracious capitulation as a tribute to his virile attractions.

'Aha! My little girl is beginning to do as I say!' and he lingered and leered over putting me into my coat. He was not merely stupid; he was repulsive. Once more in his car — a long, shiny, chrome-finished American job, I understood my role. His car and his girl — the two great symbols of bella figura. I cursed myself for my misguided kindness, for my idiocy in not seeing that, in the Dublin of the fifties, when sheer numerical imbalance of the sexes put everything in the man's favour, he could have entertained for years an absurd idea of the value of his attentions. I approached his mother's halldoor while Trevor parked the car.

I knocked, and waited. Five minutes passed, or seemed to. I ventured to knock again. Another five minutes. Then I heard what seemed to be a great shuffling of draught excluders and shifting of curtains. The flap of the letterbox was raised and an unwelcoming voice barked 'What is it?'

It was difficult to be pleasant to waspish Mrs. Ross at the best of times, but to exude charm through a letterbox was a spectacular challenge.

32

'Ruth Furlong' I bellowed through the hole, adding, 'the doctor's sister'.

The divine associations of the word 'doctor' for her nationality (English) and class (lower middle) did the trick at once. Half the double door opened.

'Come in, come in,' she said tetchily, as I waited to be invited to do just that.

It was difficult to slide sideways through the narrow opening, especially as I was encumbered with the enormous box of chocolates Trevor had given me. Mrs. Ross pounced at once.

'I hope you haven't brought me presents,' she snapped. 'Now let me tell you, I don't hold with presents. And you an orphan. It was a waste of good money to put you to doctoring, I always said. You young people have no idea.'

Nor, indeed, had I any idea what this soliloquy was about.

'Dr. Mortimer now, he's always telling me to have a rest. Sent me to another doctor, he did, and not a thing did he do for me; just asked me a lot of questions, very nosey he was, and said to go into hospital for a rest.'

So Mortimer had sent her to a shrink. Poor chap.

'Now I don't hold with the way you have to pay for the doctor. Never paid the doctor nothing in the Chapel.'

Mrs. Ross was in the habit of equating the Chapel with England. I grasped at this topic.

'How is Mr. Hicks, the Minister?'

'Mr. Hicks? Oh, he's all for the young people. I don't hold with it. And nearly every day there's a coffee morning. They all go to each other's houses and have coffee mornings for the chapel. I don't hold with it at all, the coffee.'

One of Mrs. Ross' eccentricities was a great stress on the irrelevant, as if mornings devoted to the drinking of tea or cocoa might have been acceptable. She peered at me closely, the heavy spectacles on her worn face making it more skeletal than ever.

'You'll do alright for having children; not like Dr.

Mortimer's wife, too thin, I always said, these French foreigners. You'll do alright for Trevor.'

For Trevor! Alarm had been mounting in me since the realisation that Mrs. Ross was mad, but now I felt real panic. Trevor came in, the car having been seen to, ready to concentrate on the girl.

'I was talking to your mother about Mr. Hicks, the Minister,' I said, steering into safe topics.

'Mr. Hicks! Never! It must be the Archbishop, and a cathedral wedding!'

My God, they were both mad. What was the procedure? Humour them, and get out, quick. Making for the door I said 'I don't follow, Trevor, what wedding?'

'Ah! Isn't she delightful! So shy! So young! I used to look after you when you were a little girl. I remember how we used to play games together. When you let me hold your hand tonight I knew you still loved me.'

I sat down, feeling weak, terrified, and disgusted. Only sheer determination not to let go in the presence of this diabolic pair kept me from fainting. Now I remembered Mortimer's breezy admonition earlier in the week.

'Aren't you carrying the good works a bit far; Trevor and all that? I can't stop him asking you, but someone more his own type can be found... make it quite clear, won't you?' I made it quite clear. It sounded, especially in the high-pitched voice that came out, like a line from a bad novel.

'I'm very sorry, Trevor, if I gave you the wrong impression. I have no intention of marrying you, and never had. I thought we were just two friends having an evening together.'

In the long, mad silence that followed, I could hear only a black thumping inside my head.

'You little whore' spat Mrs. Ross, and it was easier to take than Trevor's hurt, gentle, brown eyes. He held out the expensive box.

'Won't you even take the chocolates?'

Mrs. Ross, unwittingly, came to my rescue.

'Don't let her have them. Take them back to the shop!'

Out at last, I fell twice in the potholes and the mud, and vomited into the hedge. So much for the steak, the wine, and the ice-cream. I had dropped my handbag and was afraid to go back, haunted by the thought of Mrs. Ross, an animated corpse in black spectacles. Dragging a badly twisted ankle, I stumbled along, holding the railings. Two guards with strong torches approached me.

'Well, young lady? More water with it next time! Come on, we'll see you across the road.'

Need I say that Maeve, the existentialist, and Celine, the nun, the matrons and the barristers and the brides, the judiciary, the theatre, the government and the clergy, saw, or heard about, my walk from Rialto to Harcourt Street linked by two gardai. They made no mention of it. How kind people are. Other people. Not me. It was some time before I recovered, with the help of heavy Louisa and selfish Helen. And I never again did anything I didn't really want to. Not to this day.

That was twenty years ago. Recently, in America, I visited Trevor's grave. Before a headstone that said Professor Trevor Ross PhD, I laid flowers. Perhaps I should have left chocolates as well.

the latter end

Harriet O'Carroll

The two old men sat opposite each other, about seven yards apart. Each one sat beside his bed, on the same side as the bedside locker, between the bed and the low partition that was the only thing separating them from the plate glass wall. Their beds were neat and tall, round struts of serviceable steel, starched white counterpanes without line or crumple were primly folded at the corners. The two old men too, were neat and spotless, as tidied and ordered as the furniture. Mr. Martin wore a brown suit that had seen better days, and had fitted him better in those days. It was roomy around the shoulders, and the sleeves were long so that he seemed to recede and shrink inside it. It had a thin white stripe at fairly wide intervals, and there was something about the shape of the lapels which gave it nearly a period air.

Mr. McGovern on the other side looked quite modern, apart from his shirt. His shirt was of the collar-detached variety and as a rule he preferred to dispense with the collar. On Sundays he would bow to habit and struggle with studs and tie, but his everyday appearance presented his weathered old neck unadorned. He wore a grey vee-necked pullover, and a tweed sports coat with leather patches at the elbows. His trousers were grey and undistinguished, except that the right trouser leg was turned over and pinned up to prevent it trailing where his right foot had been removed.

The glass wall stretched from floor to ceiling, and behind it lay miles and miles of city and mountain and sea. The square roofs, the tall chimneys, the oval domes and pointed spires of the city spread below, an arrangement of architectural shapes and colours like a fantastic toy. Behind the jumble of cubes and lines the mountains slept in clumsy heaps against the sky. On a very clear day they could see the sea, a distant sliver of blue to the east of the city and the streets. The view changed with the seasons, it was grey or blue or winter white, or autumn tired with dusty streets and golden brown mountains. For long stretches of the winter the dark clouds loomed dour and heavy, brooding over the dwarfed houses and obliterating the curves of the mountains. On some summer days, the scene had an intensity and a blueness as if that whole wide space had been freshly washed and bleached clean in the morning sun. It was as if the brilliant vista behind the plate glass had no reality but was merely a dazzling shop window display — beautiful and untouchable.

Every morning the nurses came with basins of warm water and cups of tea, first thing in the morning before the curtains were drawn. Then gradually the ward was shaken from its silence, there were cries of 'Good morning Mr. Martin' and 'Good morning Mr. McGovern' as the day nurses came on duty. The two old men were dressed and given breakfast beside their beds. They sat still while all around them the routines of the morning were in full spate. The bed-tables and the breakfast trolley and the lockers rattled, they were surrounded by the bustle and activity of tidying, washing, bed-making, vacuum cleaning and dusting. Voices rang loud around the ward.

'Nurse, can I have a bedpan?'

'What's up with Sister this morning, she's in a right mood.'

'Didn't you hear? It's all off with Tom?'

'No! Well, I never.'

'Nurse, a bedpan!'

'Coming.'

There was a quieter space of time, later when the morning coffee came and the two men supped and brooded over it, making it last. Usually the woman from the library came to one of the old men and just about that time someone turned on the radio. The ward was filled with reports of disasters in Hong Kong, murder in the North and Balance of Trade figures. Mr. McGovern reflected that little could happen now that would alter his life, either for better or worse. There was nothing new now to either hope for or to fear. His time had become all peaceful monotony, the days succeeded each other quickly like hours, unmarked by worry or disappointment or any particular joy. There were some moments when he was stirred to a feeling of gladness, as at his grand-daughter's engagement. She had been his special favourite, his pet and confidant, but though he cared for her as much as ever, and saw her often, he found himself thinking of her in the past tense, and his pleasure in her joy was blunted and blurred. He could feel irritation and displeasure at some oversight of the nurses, but dully, as if it were an emotion observed rather than experienced.

His whole life had taken on the habit of observation. He noticed, rather than felt the time passing, the quality of his food, the increasing shortness of his breath on moving. When he woke in the morning he was conscious merely of being awake. Even the long habit of being glad that it was Saturday and sorry if it were Monday had gradually eroded. Days were no longer either good days or bad days, some were a little colder than others but even that distinction was smoothed away by the central heating.

To Mr. McGovern the only index of change was the constant but ever-variable view. He watched the change of light in the distance, the clouds moving aside to let the sun pick out the tall factory chimneys, then the church spires and finally the roofs and streets. Each time he found something new in the well-known scene, a patch of green between the houses, a row of cottages, or an unexpected tree beside the canal. As the shadows came and the clouds darkened around the mountains it was suddenly lunchtime.

'Soup? Mr. McGovern?'

'What sort?'

'Vegetable.'

'Alright.'

'More potatoes?'

'Yes, more potatoes. Thank you.'

'Tea or coffee.'

'Tea, please.'

It was always tea, and they always asked.

Mr. McGovern looked at the rain, gathering, falling and beating against the glass. The roofs gleamed wet and the copper domes shone green while the great drops spattered and streamed down the plate glass in deltas and islands dividing and reuniting until all the city was distorted and sub-aqueous. In winter the street lights came on in white and yellow lines, and shortly after, in scattered groups, the square gold patches from a thousand windows. Last of all, as blackness dominated the centre of the city, and the flashing neon lights, a red halo hung in the dark sky.

Tea time came and passed. After tea the long green curtains were pulled and the space and distance were gone as if they had never been. The night was excluded, life felt cosy and enclosed.

Now into this tight small world came the visitors, bringing with them the rustle of paper bags, the hum of desultory conversation and an impression of restlessness. They seemed like migrant birds, leaving aside for a moment their serious destination, but with muscles tensed and instincts ready for when the short detour was over. Mr. McGovern didn't have many visitors but those he had were reliable. His grand-daughter came and stuck pictures of her favourite pop stars around his bed. She filled him in on her activities. Commentaries on the dances she had been to.

'Janey, Granda, you shoulda seen the disco on Saturday. Forty fellas and thirty-five of them half cut. And the women! All of them thirty if they were a day, except for the children!'

'Children?'

'Well, young ones anyway.' 'If I hadn't me fella with me I woulda turned round and gone straight home. And the DJ! He looked as if he should be drawing the pension.'

She told him about her boy friend, and how hard it was to find somewhere to live when they got married. She said money went nowhere these days and she was thinking of changing her job, if she could get something better.

'The new supervisor, Granda, she's brutal, she saw me coming in five minutes after nine, five minutes mind you, "Are you aware of the time Miss McGovern?" she says. I had an answer for her though, "I'm on a message for Mr. Mulroy" I said. You shoulda seen how she looked. Frustration's her problem.'

She hadn't changed since she was a child, to him, at any rate. She was pretty and emphatic and he still saw her as a little girl rushing in from the street with tales of excitement and discovery. She tried to fill his life with the personalities and events of her world, talking of her friends and enemies, her hopes, plans, and opinions. He thought of it like a serial on the radio, dull in some parts and interesting in others. He seemed to himself to spend much of her visit trying to remember things he wanted to say to her, and even after she had gone he couldn't always recall them, but thought instead of comments he should have made on her last conversation. These, in their turn would haunt him on her next visit.

His son didn't come very often, but his daughter-in-law did. He remembered how she had annoyed him with her energy and go when they had lived in the same house. She disturbed the evenness of his days. She seemed to be

40

constantly tidying and improving the house, always papering or painting or moving. To him the improvement attained did not recompense for the disturbance created, but he realised that he was alone in this viewpoint. He understood that it was just as irritating for her to have an old man constantly in the way. He often thought she would like to tidy, scrub and improve even him. So it was in some ways a slight relief to have left home, to have accepted the narrowing of his world. Now he could feel grateful, gratitude was the sort of lukewarm emotion which suited him these days. He was grateful for that same energy as she came to see him, trying to make him feel still part of the family. He thought it odd that he did not envy her for her energy or enthusiasm. She cared so much about everything. She was so extremely saddened or pleased by setbacks or successes. As she talked her pleasure and pain were reflected in her face, was it his imagination that pain exceeded pleasure in anyone's experience and that the anaesthesia of age was to be welcomed rather than repelled? Even now, her face was alight with indignation, telling him of a neighbours situation.

'Would you believe it? Another baby and the youngest not gone twelve months! It's not right. How is she going to manage? And he hasn't worked for months. I tell you that woman doesn't have to die to know what Purgatory is like.'

He let her voice flow on. He considered himself fortunate that neither of his visitors demanded much from him in the way of reply. He was content to listen, and to nod agreement, letting himself be borne along on the tide of other people's lives. As the time approached for the end of her visit, his daughter-in-law began her usual litany of questions.

'Is there anything you need?'

'Do you want anything to eat?'

'Have you enough tobacco?'

'What about fruit? Do you want any apples?'

'Have you enough to read? Did you get the paper?'!

His needs were few. He smoked a little tobacco each week,

he spent more time sucking on an empty pipe than on a glowing one. He read very little. The changing scenery behind the window was more restful to his eyes and spirit than the busy lines of black print.

A double bell announced the end of visiting time, and caused a sudden flurry of noise. Again feet clattered along the parquet, voices rang around the ward, promises to come again soon, messages and wishes flew about. Bit by bit the bustle died away, the glass door swung shut after the final departing visitor and the ward fell into a weary silence. Before long the night nurse would come around with the pills, doling out sleep from little bottles. Subdued preparations for bed took place, a few murmured conversations sprang up and died away, the lights were turned out and there was nothing but the curtain of night before the following day. A day no longer seemed complete, a unit in itself starting with the dawn and concluding with night time sleep. Rather, days seemed to reach into each other and overlap like a succession of images blending on a screen.

It always seemed to Mr. McGovern that it was a sad waste to have Mr. Martin sitting beside the window. It was ironic to see him sitting there beside that beautiful view, totally untouched by it all, because he was blind. Whenever he considered it, Mr. McGovern decided that his own disability was infinitely preferable to that of Mr. Martin. A slow circulation and weak heart had cost him one foot and limited the amount of exercise he could take to a short trip to the bathroom. He retained with that a small dignifying measure of independence.

Mr. Martin was blind in the way of one to whom blindness had come quickly and late. He had not built up any compensating network of perception to allow him to move with any confidence. When still, his sharp and precise hearing enabled him to distinguish voices, incidents and personalities. It was when he tried to move that he became hesitant and bewildered, he clasped at the wall and clung to helpers as if trying to absorb security through his fingertips. Mr. Martin lived inside a small area, the space between his bed and the window, the few yards to the toilet. He knew who came in and went out of the ward, what visitors were expected on particular days. He knew every change of nurse and patient, every arrival and departure. But he accorded all this only a passing interest. He could afford them only slight attention compared with his major preoccupation.

Ailments of minor importance had grown and expanded in his mind until like a fog they excluded all but the dimmest impression of the outside world. For hours he speculated on the next visit of the chiropodist, and pondered the condition of each of his toes. He wondered was there a slight draught playing on the back of his neck, a draught which might lead to a rheumatic ache. He thought about the possibility that he had dandruff, and puzzled about whether there was enough roughage in his diet. His involvement with his physical condition did not spring from any fear of death. He was not trying to prolong life by maintaining every fibre as well as possible. It was his hobby and occupation as if his body were a pet which he spent his time feeding, grooming and pampering.

In the locker beside his bed he kept an assortment of bottles and powders, suitable for every eventuality. He had brooded on the subject of his death, which he realised could not be very distant, until the thought became boring and at this point he accepted and forgot about it. Death is unreal at any age, only as a figment of fantasy could he relate it to himself.

Mr. Martin had no doubts about an afterlife. He had complete confidence in a Heaven peopled by the saints whose unseen pictures hung around his bed. There was St. Francis of Assisi, in brown monk's habit and in conversation with a sparrow. He was a saint with whom Mr. Martin felt a sense of kinship as he was a countryman himself. There was St. Maria

Goretti, a fair haired child, and St. Augustine of Hippo, a severe looking bishop. He spoke to them in his prayers every day and expressed the wish to rejoice with them forever. But when he tried to persuade his mind to dwell on the details he hoped to gain, he found his thoughts straying to a slight ache in his left knee, or a barely felt wheeze in his chest and he would contemplate without anxiety the various panaceas at his disposal.

Each of the old men lived alone within himself. On the occasions when they emerged from their self-absorption it was to each other they turned. They exchanged leisurely sentences, lapsing into long spells of thought, and so they maintained slow conversation through the day. Mr. McGovern supplied to Mr. Martin the clues he thought he might need to complete the puzzle forced on him by his blindness.

'The dinner must be coming, Sister is after going out to see about it.'

Mr. McGovern gave a weather report, whether it was a fine or gloomy day and went into long musing reveries of other good days and bad days he had known, of how there was a time when a sunny day seemed to be an emblem of hope, a whisper about worlds to be conquered and dreams to be realised, and a dismal day seemed to be a confirmation of the world's essential sadness. And he considered now that the hope and the sadness were equally an illusion.

Occasionally they would reminisce, not about the important events of their lives, but about odd or trivial incidents, or happenings they had not understood at the time and now might never understand. Mr. Martin frequently said how strange it seemed that he, a countryman, used to the smell and feel, cold and heat, of the open air, should sit there and no difference to him between winter and summer. He remembered how the wind flung itself around the rocks and clinging houses of his homeplace. He remembered his small farm, the uneven lane up to the house, the pools of water in the yard, the cold bite of metal on his hand on a frosty morning.

He thought of his crops, the field of potatoes and cabbages, the field of oats, pale green to dark green to gold. Now the nearest he would get to growing things would be the rubber plant at the door of the ward. He thought of it, not with a sense of deprivation, but simply of wonder that his life should have taken this strange twist.

Amidst the noise of cleaning and dusting, trolley rolling and chatting there seemed to be a pool of silence between the two men in the long pauses between their sentences. In their silence their thoughts were not of wisdom or justice or the meaning of life, but the passage of clouds across the sky, of the dust in the slanting sunbeams, of the cars going up and down the streets behind the window, the click of feet on the parquet floor, the squeak of steel castors as the beds were moved.

Mr. McGovern asked Mr. Martin if he had ever suffered from such a thing as a corn. Mr. Martin replied that he had indeed and that a painful thing it had been too. After a while Mr. McGovern said that it was a strange thing that all his life he should never be troubled by such a thing and that it should come to him now.

'Aye' said Mr. Martin slowly, 'It comes in the latter end.'

moving

Catherine Slattery

'Bastard! Bastard!'

Cliona had taken all the biscuits, all that was left was a torn crinkly packet, and a few chewed ends of figroll, glutted onto the table, on her nightdress. Her face had got redder and redder and she rose up on the seat and glared at him.

'Dirty! Dirty word!' she screamed 'I'll tell mother!'

He had pushed her off the chair and they were running round and round the table, screaming, the table shook and shook until the milk splattered all over the papers and chairs and slopped into a puddle.

They stopped running and backed away, one either side of the puddle.

'Mummy says bastard.'

'She does *not*!'

'She does so! She dôes so! I heard her! She said it to Daddy. She did she did she did!'

'I'll tell! I'll tell!'

She kicked him. He kicked back, and they both fell, howling, about the kitchen floor, soggy and scratched, thrusting crumby, sticky fingers all over each other, each in turn the victim, braced to roar when the other made contact.

Their mother, working in the sitting room next door, heard the noise and came in. In a moment she had them, an arm each, and was dragging them up off the floor.

'Stop it. Both of you. *Now.*'

'Mother he. . .'

'Cliona!'

The carpet out in the corridor was rolled up and spiders were making their way across the damp floorboards.

'She . . .'

'Shh! Shh! Come on, upstairs. Up!'

They went up the stairs, along the right hand side, avoiding the boxes on the steps, rubbing along the walls. The carpet on the stairs, too, had been taken up and there was a series of marks, almost like stretch marks where the edges had been; and the patter of the feet made imprints in the dark, shallow dust.

'Stephen. Stephen, please be careful of your head. You'll knock the paintings. Stephen!'

'Ow!'

'Oh go on. Get up!'

The night was cool and fragrant, an end of summer night, breathing. From there, at the top of the house, one could smell sweet pea and meadowgrass, fruit — a kaleidoscope of summer smells weaving their way into each other, and through the house. The end of summer — humming, ticking down in the garden, and inside, shimmering, groping shadows dappling the white walls, roaming around them, incredulous.

Ten o'clock already.

'Bed.'

The children were on their knees, smelling of toothpaste, flung across the pillow. The two heads bobbed together —

'There are four corners on my bed . . .'

The words were breaking across the room, running along, past each other, into each other; crashing.

'Start it again please.'

47

She stood by the window, watching them, her arms folded around each other, keeping time with the pat-pat of her hands on her shoulders. When she stopped to gather them into bed her arms were full of the perfume of apricot tart.

'Goodnight mummy.'

In a moment they were both around her neck, hugging her. Cliona jumped down and landed on Stephen's foot.

'Ow! *Bastard*!' he howled.

'*Stephen!*'

She dropped him and stared: he had gone suddenly silent and was shuffling his feet along the floor, blushing.

'Stephen!' she slapped him and bundled them both into bed. 'Don't ever, ever say that nasty word again.'

The door clinked shut and she stood outside it, holding the handle behind her back and breathing low. Oh God, she thought, 'I'm tired.' She left the door and strolled across the landing towards her own room. She opened the door and the room was full of lilac light and easy smells, but it was already beginning to be damp, and would soon be musty. There were suitcases and boxes piled high, half labelled, half-closed. She walked towards the bed, her fingers strolling along the table, chest, lamps. Her feet were sore. Children, oh but they remember the most amazing things. But then, it couldn't be helped. Lord, how things had changed. Over a year ago now, another summer, receding.

It had been the night of the fireworks. A nation celebrating its liberation. At home, tired, he had begun to beat her, beating, thrashing out as hard as he could, and she couldn't move. When he had finally fallen asleep she had managed to stumble down the stairs to reach the telephone, the folds of her dress soggy with blood, and vomit. The next morning, her head swathed in bandages, she had made her way through the antiseptic corridors and taken a bus to a solicitor's office.

He was dressed in a crumpled linen suit. A little foreigner

sitting behind a pile of documents, he had turned off the fan on his desk when she began to speak. Hordes of flies had come in through the blinds and were buzzing around her head and the solicitor had poured her a drink and asked her to sit down. The Irish, they always loved whiskey, yes? He smiled at her, and as he clinked the ice-cubes into the glass her hand loosened on the arm of the chair, and she relaxed. He had been factual, sympathetic, and by late afternoon had managed to draft divorce proceedings, reassure her. He walked her along the corridor and shook her hand, gesticulating, promising her rights in a myriad of paragraphs and quotes. Women have rights in this country, he told her.

When she got home Cliona and Stephen were still playing in the limetrees, down by the river. She pushed the back-door open quietly and slipped inside, on tiptoes. Across the drawing room she could see his shadow on the porch, drinking, rocking slowly on the canopy. The floorboards creaked and he turned towards her and stood up.

'Elizabeth?'

He was sobbing. 'Elizabeth . . .'

He was inside now too, opposite her, and she backed away.

'My God! Look at you. I am so sorry.'

He was moving towards her slowly, groping, hunched.

She moved towards the backdoor —

'Please. Don't.'

'My God. Elizabeth I was drunk. Look. Look Elizabeth will you look at me please. Elizabeth!'

She was going through the door and she pushed it open, slamming it back against the porch.

'I'm so sorry.'

'Yes. And the last time and the time before that too.' Her hands were clenched by her sides.

'Get out!' she said.

Night after night he had called to her, coming all around the windows, unable to get in. Night after night after night he came back, pleading, contrite. It had gone on too long. She

49

never answered. Then, on a very hot night, he had hacked his way through the porch with a hatchet, reeking of whiskey, screaming that he wanted to kill her. She had run into the children's bedroom, bolted the door, and waited behind it, shivering. All the old photographs had been smashed downstairs, the windows broken. In the morning the solicitor had picked his way through the smashed, crinkling glass and told her it would be alright, she had enough to get a court injunction against him. She had. Yes, it would be done as quickly as possible. By the end of the week it would be granted. Nothing in the house, or in any of their property, anywhere, could be touched by him, taken by him. He was not to approach her, nor her children. The injunction would take effect on the following Monday, at noon.

At nine o'clock on the Monday morning she awoke to the sound of lorries on the driveway. She came downstairs in her dressing gown to see her husband supervise the removal from the front hall. Clocks, pictures, lacquered chests, wedding gifts and honeymoon vases, the piano, the carpets, even her persian rug, beds, silver, wardrobes, garden chairs, linen, everything. Every single blessed thing. He hadn't worked for nothing, had he. It was his. Everything. And the children? They were hers. There was money for them. Everything. Packed. Gone. She stood on the porch watching the last of it being driven away.

'You bastard' she said, and that was all she could say, over and over. Over and over, and he was gone.

By twelve o'clock Cliona was hanging from her belt, asking where Daddy was. Stephen was sitting on a window ledge, wide-eyed, watching. She spent the whole day there, staring. She couldn't move. Everything. Nothing. Hollow.

Ten days later she had arrived in Ireland, complete with three new suitcases full of clothes, and two tired children. They had taken a bus out to Saggart to the old house, and the children had whispered on the landing and played. They

climbed up into the attic and began taking
chairs. Gradually the old house grew habitable
was still summer.

If nothing else it was safe. She set about organi
for the children and some work for herself. She
type. Her children were happy and each night, as a
would open the door of their bedroom, and in a shaf
would kiss them. They visited her mother, and after th
sobbing, week by week she would watch relations g
children tenpences and gasp and nod and tuttut unt
believed she would burst. She began to understand that
huge anchor of their various sympathies would eventua
weigh her down, and she knew that she couldn't come bac.
Things had changed. She just couldn't.

The news eventually filtered through, as it always will,
that he, too, had come back. She felt a pang, a longing to
move on. Out. Somewhere bright. Somewhere away from the
drizzle and depression, the never-ending run of wellwished
afternoon teas. The children had settled happily into school,
they had people who were their own age now, playmates. All
through the holidays they chattered on, lapping and wriggling,
in tales of secret seven gangs climbing rusty, cobweb towers at
midnight hours, discovering secret passages.

At least he didn't come near them. That, they had been
spared. She wondered how long it would last, but mainly she
just rocked in front of the television and thanked God. She
had stopped work early in the summer, and organized the
ticket and visa, the sale of the things she couldn't send on
ahead of her, or take with her.

One evening his brother had come to visit. He ran his finger
along the mantlepiece and reminisced about the old times,
before they left. The summer parties in Saggart, nobody would
miss one! After a while she asked him what he wanted. His
brother had been hospitalized, he said, dried out, you know?
She knew, it had happened before. He shook his head. He
wouldn't be released for some time yet. He had no job, of

se, nowhere to live. Of course he could stay with his ily for a while, that was only natural after all. Of course. d the children, they would be going back to school soon? s. Lovely children, lovely children. Yes. His brother had no bjection to them living in the house, they had to settle in omewhere, indeed, indeed. She did know that the house was n his brother's name? She did realise that, in fact, it was his house? And she understood that when he was released . . .

She stood up very slowly and asked him to leave. His solicitors . . . She knew, she knew and would he please get out. He left and she slammed the door.

It was morning already, and she was lying on the bed, still in her clothes. The sun had come up, but there was a breeze whipping its way around the house. Cliona and Stephen would soon be moving about, chattering. She got up and began sealing the last of the boxes. She had a shower and changed her clothes, wrapping the old ones and stuffing them into the last available corner in her suitcase. She woke the children and watched them wriggle into their school uniforms for the first time since June. They had grown again over the summer, and would soon be needing new ones. As they packed their books and teddy bears she wandered around the house wrapping the last of the paraphernalia, etchings and sheet music, plastic buckets, china.

The taximan was on time, and she thanked him for it. It was almost dark as they left the house, closing out the door with a hollow bang. The taximan was helpful, and strapped Stephen and the suitcases and boxes into the back of the car with equal energy and good humour. The long grass was already beginning to cover the flower beds, the steps, the windows were bolted shut, some cracked, all silent. There was nothing at all left inside but a series of still shadows, stipple on a broad, white canvas. They drove down the road quickly, Stephen and Cliona waving through the back windows.

'Goodbye our house,' they called, sucking toffees.

She sat in the front of the car with her handbag
knee, open, checking ticket, passport, lipstick. It was
beginning to rain. Soon they had arrived at the gates into the
school and the children began hopping up and down excitedly.
The avenue was long and narrow, shaded on all sides by long,
leafy trees and September smoke, trickling through the
evening skyline at each new bend. The building was already
full of bright, yellow light. The taxi came to a stop and she
got out and took out the children's suitcases:

'Remember not to fight. Be good now.'

They clambered around the old oak doorway, ringing
madly, shouting.

'Stephen. Cliona. Stop!'

'Oh mummy, mummy!'

They ran at her, leaping up, arms flung around her neck,
kissing everything they came in contact with, shrieking.

'Shh! Shh. . . shh. You'll come out to see me at Christmas.'

'And we'll go swimming?'

'Yes. We'll all go swimming!'

They had buried their heads in her coat. She hugged them
and sat down on her heels. She stood them both in front of
her and held their hands, speaking very slowly.

'Now remember' she said, 'remember what you have to
tell daddy. Tell him that mummy has gone away. Tell daddy
that he can go back to his house in Saggart now. Tell him
that.' And she kissed them, and left.

53

an old woman of the home

Bernadette Quinn

Ann Dillon rang the door-bell and waited. She rang it again. There was a shuffling sound and dragging, heavy footsteps came down the hallway. After some fumbling the door was opened cautiously and a face peered out. Its frame was a mass of untidy grey hair flashed with red, the eyes screwed-up and the mouth crooked.

'Yes?' it said.

'I'm Ann Dillon. Did Father Hopkins tell you I'd be calling?'

'Yes, he did.' There was no enthusiasm in the voice.

Ann smiled, though she felt like saying: It's alright. I know when I'm not wanted. Goodbye.

There was no answering smile: 'Come in.'

Miss Adams hobbled back, one hand leaning heavily on a stick. Ann stepped into the hallway, closed the door and followed her into the sitting-room. She waited until the old woman manoeuvred herself into her armchair before sitting down. Miss Adams rested her heavy black stick against the arm of the chair, pulled the small, round table close to her and peered over at her.

'Father Hopkins told me you could do with
now and again for a chat or do some messages, thin
that.'

Miss Adams reached for a packet of cigarettes from the
table. One hand was useless. Ann Dillon had forgotten that the
old woman was partially disabled.

'You have no idea how lonely some of these better-off
people can be,' Father Hopkins had told her, his round eyes
earnest behind dark-rimmed glasses. 'They'll never let on,
they're so proud.'

Miss Adams did not offer her a cigarette or ask if she
smoked. A box of matches was placed between the shiny red-
blue deformed hand and the thin chest. With the healthy hand
she drew a match three times across the side of the box before
it lit. She inhaled slowly before nestling into the lumpy
cushions that lined the back of the chair.

'Why don't you use a cigarette lighter?' Some day she's
going to set fire to herself with those matches, the visitor
thought. 'It would be handier.'

'Ah, they're more of a nuisance than anything else. There's
always something going wrong with them.'

The old woman's green jumper and brown tweed skirt went
well with the dark eyes. The legs were thin, well-shaped,
mottled by the fire and rooted loosely in brown leather boots.
The visitor felt a wave of pity for Miss Adams, but she did not
think she was going to like her and it seemed Miss Adams with
her silence and indifference felt the same way about her.

The clock on the mantelpiece struck three. Miss Adams
caught her looking at her watch. The one half-closed eye
seemed to mock her.

'It's twenty minutes fast. I like it that way.'

The visitor looked around the room. It was wallpapered in
a coffee and cream design, the colours matching the carpet
and curtains; bookshelves were on both sides of the fireplace

'Father Hopkins told me you could do wit
'I have plenty.'
'I thought you might like someone to pop in
that.'

match the armchairs backed onto the bay ... was a television set in a corner near the ... a china-cabinet facing the fireplace.

... can go anytime you like,' the old woman said.

... Ann smiled. 'I know that. I'm not here to stay, don't ... worry.'

A long stem of ash threatened to fall on the jumper. She moved her hand and flicked it into the grate where a fine sprinkling of ash indicated that the heavy green glass ash-tray on the table was more ornamental than useful. She lit a fresh cigarette.

Ann searched round in her mind for something to say but each time an idea came, anticipating Miss Adams' reaction, she let it go. The built-up fire collapsed sending a shower of sparks up the chimney and a red-hot coal onto the hearth-rug. Ann grabbed the tongs and flung the coal into the fire, swept the ash from the rug and brushed the hearth. She noticed scorch marks on the hearth-rug. If Miss Adams wasn't burned to death by setting herself alight with her cigarette-smoking, coals shooting from the fire would do the job. She sat back into her chair.

'You'd really want a fire-guard. Apart from the danger look what it's doing to your rug.'

Miss Adams allowed herself a tiny smile: 'The hearth-rug has seen better days.'

'Aren't you afraid the place might go on fire some day?'

'It does pass my mind but worrying about it won't help.'

I give up, the visitor thought. 'You could do with a fire-guard,' she said instead.

'I suppose I could.'

'Would you like to come for a drive some day?'

'Anything is better than looking at the four walls of the room.'

The tongue was sharp, the visitor observed. I just wonder if you do have that many visitors, she was thinking, but she said instead, 'If it is fine the next time I call I'll bring you for

56

a drive. Would you like to go for a walk as well?'

'I don't go out nowadays. The last time I was out I fell crossing the main road. The old boots, you know. I find it hard to get a pair that suit me. I have one pair that fit but they have laces.' She pointed to the ones she was wearing. 'They're handy. You just slip your feet into them.'

And your feet could slip as easily out of them, the visitor thought. I'm not surprised you fell if you were wearing them.

'I'll put the laced ones on before you go out and take them off when you come in. Where are they?' she said.

'Under the stairs.'

Miss Adams threw her cigarette butt into the fire. Ann got up to go. The old lady struggled to raise herself.

'Don't get up. I'll see myself out. See you Tuesday.'

'Alright. Goodbye.' The high, thin, rasping tone followed her to the hall.

Next time the visitor had to knock on the window before the shuffling, scraping sound was heard. Alert eyes looked at her as the door was opened the cautious body-width.

'I think I nodded off for a few minutes while I was watching the television.'

'You'll be all the fresher for our little run, then.'

'Ah, I don't think I'll go out today.'

Ann watched the ritual of her making herself comfortable. She said: 'It's a lovely day. The fresh air would do you good.'

'It might do me more harm than good.'

'Aren't you feeling well?'

'I'm feeling as well as I'll ever be.'

She took the cigarette packet from the table. On the table were three paper-backs, a small box of paper-tissues, the green ash-tray, rosary beads, and sweets that trailed from a paper bag.

'I had a bad night last night.'

'I'm sorry to hear that.'

The old woman stretched her good leg and gazed into the fire. The room was unchanged. The cushions were still lumpy, the same bright coal fire. But, Miss Adams had changed her clothes. She was wearing a golden mohair jumper and a brown and orange skirt.

'I like your jumper. And your skirt. The colours suit you.'

The good eye and the half-closed eye seemed to dance.

'I used to have nice clothes once. I had carrot-red hair and with the brown eyes I used to find it a challenge getting clothes to match my colouring.'

'Your hair hasn't lost all the red colour.'

'No.' She turned her face to the visitor. 'I had a temper to match but that's gone.'

'I wouldn't bet on it!'

Miss Adams looked pleased.

'I fell out of bed last night,' she said after a long silence.

Ann burst out laughing, but instead of the old lady being indignant she smiled.

'How did you manage that?'

'It comes easy now.'

'What happened?'

'Absentmindedness. I like to leave my stick against the locker where I can reach out to get it with my good hand. But last night I left it against the bed, so when I stirred in the bed it fell and when I reached down to get it I fell out onto the floor and, whatever way I fell I couldn't lever myself up and it must have been a half-hour before I got back into bed.'

She was smiling now at the thought of it, but the old lady must have been frightened. She had courage.

'How do you feel now, Miss Adams, with the sea air in your lungs?' Ann asked as they walked along the sea-front. It was Miss Adams' first day out for over a year.

'The sea smells a bit healthier than it sometimes does. Often a malodorous whiff from it comes all the way up to my front door.'

'Does it feel good to be out and walking?'

58

'It does.'

They walked slowly, Miss Adams with head down, watchful.

Now and again she paused to look out to sea. Softly curved, delicately shaded clouds rested on the horizon. The sun shone on a calm sea but the air was cold. Cars in the parking space faced out to sea.

Ann said: 'These people stuck in their cars. Why do they bother coming here when all they do is to let down a window about two inches. They haven't the stamina you and I have.'

Miss Adams looked up at the row of cars and smiled. A few people walked rapidly by or climbed up on the grassy slopes to pass them. An elegantly dressed elderly lady came towards them smiling:

'Ah, Pauline, it's good to see you.'

Miss Adams looked up.

'Hello Jane. This is Mrs. Dillon. Mrs. Dillon, Mrs. Turner.'

Ann shook hands with the gracious, smiling lady.

Mrs. Turner said 'We haven't seen you for ages, Pauline. You don't know how pleased I am to see you out.' She turned to Ann: 'She's looking well, isn't she?'

Ann said: 'I think, Miss Adams, you always look well.'

'Yes, she does, doesn't she? I don't know how she manages it. The rest of us aren't so lucky.' She laughed. 'Well, I won't delay you. I must call in to see you, Pauline, one of these days.'

'Do that. I'm not a hundred miles away.'

Mrs. Turner shot her a quick look, then laughed again. 'You're right. Goodbye, Pauline. Goodbye, Mrs. Dillon.'

'Does she call in often?' Ann asked out of earshot.

'That woman? She hasn't called in two years.'

'Where does she live?'

'At the end of the avenue.'

'You're a tough nut,' said Ann.

There was a quiet chuckle from the bowed head.

Every Sunday after Mass the parish priest came over to greet the two of them. The old woman was a regular with her now.

'And how are you, Ma'am?' he would say, looking at Miss Adams.

'Not too bad, thank you, Monsignor.'

'It's well and fresh you're looking.' He would dart an incurious glance at Ann. 'Well and fresh.'

Already his eyes had lost interest. They roamed the last few stragglers leaving the church.

'Some day,' Ann said, 'you should tell him you're not a ma-am but that you haven't given up hope.'

Miss Adams giggled. 'I'd like to see his face then.'

'I must have been the first woman who owned a motorbike in this country,' the old woman announced suddenly one day. 'After I left training college I taught in Donegal and I used to cycle home to Leitrim every weekend, come rain or shine.'

She was silent for a long time. Ann saw her, long hair flying like a bright red flag behind her as she sped through the Donegal countryside.

'When I got polio — it wasn't called that in those days — they thought I'd never make it but I recovered as much as I could. And to think all the warnings people gave me about my bike. That I'd end up some day in a million bits because of the chances I took.'

'Why didn't you ever get married?'

The younger woman knew she might answer or she might not.

Miss Adams was amused. 'Why did you get married?'

'I fell in love. I suppose that was the main reason.'

'Well, I never fell in love. That's the main reason.'

She bent down and poked the fire. Flames galloped up the chimney. She watched them for a moment, then slowly left down the long brass poker. Ann expected her to continue talking but the old lady had finished.

The only family photograph in the sitting-room was one of a young boy and girl: a nephew and niece. She talked about them. She had reared the boy, who was ten years older than his sister; that had been during the war when his parents had sent him from London to Ireland.

'Ann said: 'Didn't you like men?'

'I have nothing against them. Though I had two specimens as brothers who might put anyone off marrying.' She smiled. 'They thought they could boss me around. I remember Tom, he was the older brother, saying on my first morning home for the Christmas holidays: "Thank God Polly's here to get our breakfast." He used to call me Polly because he knew I hated that name. My mother would be working in the shop at that hour of the morning and the housekeeper wasn't ever one to attend to us hand and foot, so I said: "If you think I'm going to be your slave you have another think coming." ' The memory of the incident gave warmth to the monotonous, rasping voice. ' "You'll get your own breakfast and polish your own shoes and do all your own jobs from now on." '

The old lady's life was one on which people, her parents first of all, then her brothers, relatives and friends had always imposed, it seemed to the visitor. Yet she did not sound like a martyr. Nor was she bitter. Everything was recalled with great detail, colour and a glint of humour. Occasionally, her use of particular adjectives and phrases brought to the surface the teacher she once was.

'You have led a full life. You should write about it. Even for the fun of it.'

The brown eyes twinkled. 'I flatter myself I could always keep children amused by making up stories for them, but thinking I can write, that's a different thing entirely.'

'Well, why don't you write stories for children? If you could make them up all you have to do is to put them down on paper.'

'I could make them up alright but that was when my nephew stayed with me and he and his young friends would sit around the fire here.'

Tears welled into her eyes. They should have spilled down her cheeks but she was soon in control.

'Why did you have to look after your parents?' Ann asked.

'It was expected of me.'

'You mean your parents expected you and you having had polio?'

'It was taken for granted long before that.'

'And didn't it make any difference that you were disabled?'

'None whatever.' After a pause. 'Who else would have looked after them?'

'Your brothers, of course.'

'Humph. They weren't able to look after themselves. Joe never got married and until the day he died he was a full-time job. Drink.'

Her frankness and amused tolerance hid what must have been a coming to terms with fate. Ann thought of the hot-tempered, self-willed person who had never been free to go her own way. And when she was, finally, free, old age and bad health shackled her to the four walls of her home. Though she had grown fond of Miss Adams, the old woman gave no sign of returning affection. She did not even show disappointment if for some reason a visit had to be cancelled or shortened.

'As long as I can make Mass on Sunday,' Miss Adams would say to her, 'I don't worry about anything else.'

But there are other things as well as Mass on Sunday, Ann wanted to tell her, half believing it. Everything and every-one seemed to have let her down. Perhaps, she thinks my visits are a salve for an uneasy conscience, thought the visitor. In the beginning, perhaps, but not now. Could one tell her that? And even if it could be explained would it mean anything to her? And supposing she came to rely on her was there any guarantee that some day when she would need her most that she wouldn't let her down, too?

But Miss Adams was making sure that she did not have to rely totally on anyone.

'You won't have to bring me to Mass on Christmas Day, Mrs. Dillon. You and your husband will have enough on your hands.'

'That's nonsense. The very day we have plenty of time. Of course we'll call for you.'

Miss Adams was smiling. With pride she said, 'Two friends are calling for me. They're bringing me to a late Mass and afterwards driving me to my cousins for the Christmas dinner.'

'Oh. That's all right so. But you did come to Mass with us on Christmas Day last year.'

'I know. Tell the children thanks again for the presents. There was a visitor in when they called and I don't think I paid as much attention to them as I should have.'

'See you after Christmas then.'

Miss Adams was not at home when Ann called to her house. She presumed she was staying with the relations she had mentioned until the New Year though it was not like her to stay away so long from home. There was no reply when she phoned a few days later and when she called to the house Miss Adams was not there. The obvious thing to do, she thought, was to enquire about her from a neighbour, but the old lady might not thank her for interfering. Her relations with neighbours were not the warmest. She phoned Father Hopkins.

'Didn't you hear? Miss Adams had a stroke on Christmas Day. They had to break a window to get into the house. They found her unconscious on the kitchen floor.'

'Is she bad?'

'She's not dying if that's what you mean. She is even recovering but that's the end of her living on her own.'

'Why wasn't I told?'

'I thought you knew. Everybody knows.'

Miss Adams was sitting up, dressed, on the straight-backed chair beside her bed in the hospital ward so absorbed in her book that Ann had to tap her on the shoulder. For the first time in their relationship she was greeted with a welcoming smile.

Ann said: 'I heard you were trying to kill yourself.'

'It didn't come off.'

The dark eyes shone with merriment. Ann sat on the edge of the bed and took the old lady's hand: 'A cat with nine lives, that's what you are. Here, I've got some cigarettes for you. You still have that smoker's cough?'

'I'll bring it with me to my grave, please God.'

There were seven beds in the ward, two of them screened off. Miss Adams' bed was inside the door and the patient beside her seemed to be very old and dying. She lay, eyes closed, propped up by fat pillows. The skin, red and grey in patches was taut over the cheek-bones and the pale scalp showed through the thin white hair.

Ann turned away.

Miss Adams said: 'They thought she wouldn't make the night.'

'Why don't they pull a screen around her. It must upset you to look at her.'

'It doesn't then. Death comes to us all.'

Two days later the change in Miss Adams shocked her. The eyes, always so alive that one forgot the twisted face and wrinkled skin, were glazed with a hopeless, haunted look.

'What's wrong?'

There was no warning. Tears poured in torrents down the old cheeks; the dam that had held so fast through the years had burst. Ann put her arms around her.

The old lady sobbed for a long time, the sobbing punctuated by incoherent apologies. Conversation stopped between a patient opposite and her two visitors as they looked on, quietly curious.

A nurse swept into the ward, turned her head in Miss

Adams' direction but went to another patient. Miss Adams moved her head from Ann's chest, blew her nose, shook her head and blew her nose again.

'Please tell me.'

'I wet the bed last night. I called for the bed-pan and no one came and then I wet the bed.'

'Is that all? Don't worry. The nurses are used to that.'

'It never happened me before.'

Tears were beginning to flow again.

Ann said: 'So what? Tell me, do you like it here?'

Miss Adams looked around the ward. There was no fellow-feeling for the other patients in her eyes.

'No, I don't.'

Another nurse came into the ward and over to Miss Adams. She smiled: 'And how are you today?'

'Not that wonderful.'

'But you said that yesterday and last week and look at the way you're improving. You're walking now with only one nurse helping you.'

The nurse put her arm around her and ruffled her hair: 'Cheer up. I'll be around to see you later.'

'She's nice,' Ann said when the nurse left.

'They're all nice. Oh, but what's going to happen to me when I leave here?' Miss Adams was crying again. 'What's going to happen to me?'

So that's the reason for the break-down, Ann thought.

'They want me to go to a nursing-home. I can't afford the good ones and I know what the others are like. I wouldn't let them put my father and mother into one. They died at home. I wouldn't put a dog into some of those nursing-homes, so I wouldn't. What's going to happen to me at all?'

'Have you got in touch with your nephew?'

'Gerard doesn't know I'm in hospital. I don't want to worry him.'

'Well, it's time he was worried. Supposing one of the neighbours gets in touch with him how do you think he'll feel then?'

'The doctor wants to get in touch with him but I won't let him.'

'You're being very foolish.'

Miss Adams clawed the coverlet of the bed: 'I have never bothered him before.'

'It's time you did.'

Ann was beginning to dislike this nephew, well-off, married and childless. Finally the old lady agreed.

'I'll ring Gerard this evening so.'

'Good. Between the three of us we'll come up with something.'

Miss Adams sat in her chair near the window, reading. Now and again she raised her eyes at the sound of footsteps on the gravelled front. Sometimes she put the book aside, took off her glasses and let her eyes wander around the garden.

There was one thing to be said for the place and it was about the only thing; it had a nice garden and although it wasn't kept as well as it could be it had a good sweep of lawn and some fine trees and shrubs. Clumps of daffodils showed here and there. A blackbird hopped warily, keeping close to the hedge, then arrowed for the nest that she was sure was in that shrub, what's this it was called? She had one at home. Ah, yes, *Senecio Laxifolius.* That was it. It was a nice shrub but it would spread all over the place if you let it. She liked to look at it when it was covered with golden daisy-flowers. If only she could get out and walk to the shrub and see if there was a nest there.

She remembered the first time she showed Gerard a bird's nest. She could still see the look of wonderment and tenderness on his face as he watched the three fledglings, beaks opening so wide it looked as if their ugly little heads would turn inside out. He had left her for a minute and returned holding a thin, wriggling worm which he wanted to drop into a gaping beak. She had to explain how he mustn't touch the nest or the babies. Only look.

If only she could exercise her leg more she would be able to get out into the fresh air, take a walk round the garden, but they never bothered here helping her with her exercises. Thank God she was getting out of this place tomorrow. Gerard had got her a nice place on the sea-front. She would have a room to herself facing the sea and be better looked after. She'd never feel it, he told her, until she was back in her own house. She couldn't get out of this place fast enough. Call it a nursing-home? There were five beds in the room and it was smelly and untidy and it looked as if the tall windows had never been opened. And if that weren't bad enough she had a senile, legless patient beside her who would scold the other patients at odd times, or ask them for combs and hair-clips so as to have her hair nice for her visitors. The visitors that never came.

The same patient, when the notion took her, scolded Mrs. Dillon for coming at the wrong time, urging her in whispers to leave before the meals came in. She wondered would Mrs. Dillon call this evening. Mrs. Dillon never, at anytime, looked on her as a helpless old woman, never spoke about her as if she, Pauline Adams, wasn't there, or worse, wasn't quite all there. She looked forward to Mrs. Dillon's visits. She hadn't that many visitors but as long as she had a good supply of books, Gerard's letters and his interest in her welfare she wasn't too badly off. Gerard and Mrs. Dillon. Knowing those two would never let her down she had insisted on going to a nursing-home after she left hospital.

No matter what they said she wouldn't have liked to be a burden on either of them. But she'd love to get back to her own house, sit by her own fireside and look at her own television. No matter how good the other nursing home would be — and Gerard, who had seen it, was full of praise for it — it could never make up for her own home. But it wouldn't be long now.

Ann Dillon parked the car in the driveway of the nursing home, her mind taken up with Gerard's plans. Tomorrow he was taking his aunt to the new nursing home where he had arranged for her to stay permanently. There was no question of her ever going back to her house but his aunt did not know this yet. Some day he would have to tell her because the house would have to be sold and her affairs put in order. It was sad but that was life.

As she climbed the steps to the front door Ann thought of the little old lady. Sitting. Waiting. The stale smell of cooking was in the hall. The dusty, brown oil-painted walls depressed her. She felt like crying.

Miss Adams turned her head from the window as she opened the door and a smile lit up her face: 'Ah, Mrs. Dillon, I was hoping you'd come today.'

paper roses

Ann McKay

She felt all wrong, and kept one finger trailing on the wall as she walked down the hill. The finger hurt, and she knew it was all wrong. The way she walked in her shoes, with elasto-plast stuck in each heel to stop them rubbing, you could tell they were new. Brogues were in that year and gunsmoke grey tights. Her tights were gunsmoke grey and her new shoes were brogues, but they had laces.

'They'll do you for school as well,' her mother had said, and mute with disappointment, she couldn't look at her feet. And the tights weren't right either, for the grey showed up all the blonde hairs that came through. She had tried to push them under, then tried plucking them out with tweezers but she hadn't had time.

'I'll have to do,' she whispered, miserable and fierce, 'I'll just have to do.'

Under her coat she felt fine. Blue knee-length swingy skirt and bluey grey smock with ritzy black buttons on the cuffs. She was proud of her young breasts as they poked the smock into folds. She must remember to hold her shoulders back, keeping the bust in its pink nylon bra well to the fore. She had

69

put talc on her bosom, rolled deodorant in her shaven under-arm hollows, more talc between the legs and in the shoes. A speck of perfume on her throat, behind the ears and on the arms. And then the face. Foundation, misty beige, working its smug magic as she smoothed the pale bloom upwards and out-wards on her cheeks, blending carefully to erase the seam of colour. Marks on chin and forehead were doused with astringent, and then smeared over with chalky spot-stick. She moved her face as she worked, nodding like a sparrow in a privet hedge, angling towards the mirror.

'Now,' she said, like you would to a baby or a sick person, 'now we'll do the eyes.' And she took a small flat cake of powder in a clear plastic box from a selection on the dressing table. Blue jade, to go with her skirt. She dabbed her eyelids vaguely with a powdery fingertip, and looked. The effect was more startled than startling. Her eyes seemed bigger and suddenly wide, almost frightened. She evaded their plea, twisting away from the mirror. And saw on her bed, amidst the customary litter of her Fridays, beside a Mars bar wrapper and a *Loving* magazine, innocuous as a very personal secret or a very private joke, a small brown paper bag.

Holding her lower lip with her top teeth, she lifted the bag with fingertips and opened it, letting the receipt fall on the carpet. Not that the contents were especially breathtaking. Just a small cluster of artificial flowers, dusty purple rosebuds, five, and two paper green leaves. Involuntarily, she raised them to her face and sniffed. And there was a smell. Like ashes of roses, essence of honeysuckle, moonwind and apple blossom, rapture and l'aimant, the names on bottles, the new scent of her own body. She suddenly felt lovely and the night ahead was full of promise. Slowly and happily she unscrewed the lid of another small jar and took out a safety pin. Facing the mirror she positioned the roses with her left hand, moving them from left to right, looking down to make sure, and pinned them by their wiry stalks to the warm cloth over her left breast. She peered once more in the mirror, a strange new smile peered back.

'Well, gorgeous,' she whispered. 'You'll do.'

But that was then and now, standing on her own at the bus stop, she wasn't so sure. She was waiting for her friend from school, but the crowd on the bus couldn't know that. They would think she'd been stood up. Five to eight and she still hadn't come. The bus would be leaving any minute, and you couldn't go to a dance on your own, not a girl anyway, it would be like a lamb walking into a butcher's shop with mint in its teeth.

At eight o'clock the driver folded his newspaper and started the engine of the bus. He had a gold tooth at the front when he smiled at her.

'Right, dear. Are you coming or going or what are you doing?' The motor growled.

She looked up the road and down, as if for an answer. A cool breeze swept the street and she felt her breasts stiffen beneath her coat. She reached out and grabbed the shiny cold handrail.

'Wait,' she said. 'I'm going.'

The bus was full. It was one of those long narrow buses that do the slow run around Donegal twice a day. During the daytime the seats have a strictly serviceable aspect, crammed behind each other, dark green baize and stiff-backed where labourers sit in black jackets, unmoved by the scenery and smoking the miles away, the women with their chainstore shopping in plastic carriers slumped on their knees. The girl was almost surprised, as she stood expectantly in the narrow aisle, not to smell the sweat and dust on clothes, or fresh food in paper bags. But this was long past the end of the working day, and the wishful heavy scent of cigarettes and shampooed hair and bottled beer and aftershave went to her head in an overwhelming confirmation of her most secret longings. All she could see in the smoky fog was a sward of hair and a crowd of faces, pale and raucous. She could feel the excitement, it was tangible, like the warm sweat of breath condensing on the windows.

There were no seats at the front, so the girl shoved and clambered down to the back of the bus, where a skinny youth in denims sprawled with his legs on the seat and his head against the grimy windows. He had the face of a plucked chicken, with a few hairs on his cheeks and chin, and milky blue eyes looking nowhere. There was a torn six-pack between his legs, and a bottle lolled and tipped in one hand. She hesitated, wondering whether to risk safety by interrupting his reverie, or dignity by standing for the rest of the journey, until an attentive clean-shaven man in a tight grey suit jumped to his feet and gave her a capable grin.

'Come on, Skinner,' he said, delivering a smart clip on the ear for emphasis. 'Shift yer arse and give the lady a seat.'

She moved back to let him pass and as the six-pack touched between their chests, Skinner smiled, a long thin watery smile.

'That's a nice bunch of flowers,' he said.

She took the seat with careful good grace, settling herself for the journey with smoothed skirt and combed hair. She looked out the window, seeing nothing of the night but the faces and bodies of the people around her, and in the midst of the motion picture, her own face. She looked pleased. She looked ready and willing for anything. She was and she knew it and couldn't keep from smiling, even though the Skinner in the window was smiling back, from where he perched on the knee of two shaggy-haired girls. He took a bottle from his pack and passed it, uncapped and foaming, across the passage. She bit her lip.

'Go on,' he said. 'Treat yourself.'

So she took his gift with thanks, knowing as she tried to sip without choking or dribbling or breaking her teeth, that he was leering at her still, winking and toasting in the novelty of his patronage. She didn't mind, it wasn't as if he was all over her, and she ignored him. There was a stop after half an hour for more six-packs, the driver hadn't either the heart or the nerve to refuse, and frequent stops after that in the mountains, where all the girls but one pressed their faces against the windows, peering to see the rows of boys standing with their backs to the bus, greeting them with jeers as they stepped up into the lighted door, red-faced and grinning, rubbing their hands.

She clasped her hands in her lap, and wished they were there. She wanted to be there, and to know what it was like again, to be drunk and in love and dancing. Without the same old gossipy schoolday faces, the coke and crisps and yoyo biscuits served by kindly youth workers, and the same top twenty records played over and over in irritating disorder. Tonight there would be over eighteens and smoking and drinking and a live group with dancing until one. She had read the advertisement in the paper so many times, she had schemed and planned and dreamed herself into a trance of expectation. She sat now in silence, tapping one foot despite herself with the roaring and whistling, she leaned back against the stiff-backed seat with closed eyes, tracing with careful fingers the flimsy petals and papery leaves of her roses.

Singing and stamping, the busload swung into the carpark of the dancehall. It was a long building like a Dutch barn, illuminated on the outside by a lowslung line of coloured light bulbs. Music glared into the night like the searchlights on the coast beyond, with Scotland on the east and on the west, America.

The three bouncers, in pink shirts and red dickie bows, flexed and watched with arms folded as the bus emptied before the door. One of them, the smallest, stood just beyond the ticket desk, wiping a flap of fair hair back onto his forehead. It flapped back. He licked his lips. The other two stood hulking and chewing gum on either side of the entrance, kicking with stacked heels at a cardboard placard, *No Denims*. They looked as if they meant it.

The men from Derry took the hint and started pulling ties from the pockets of their good suits, but Skinner in his Wranglers was apprehended at the door and steered in a no-

nonsense manner back towards the bus. Encouraged by the sympathetic jeers of his mates, he made a token resistance, crestfallen and clowning, upstaging his disappointment with half-hearted gyrations and muttered blasphemies. The bouncers left him with a paternal shove, and Skinner stood his ground, brandishing a full bottle of Mundies, head tilted like a fire-eater, he poured the wine down his throat from a showy height. But the commiseration was non-commital, and no-one noticed, as they all shifted and shuffled into an orderly queue, in pairs and packs and dressed to kill.

Once inside, the girls all headed for the ladies' cloakroom. Coats off, they jostled for places at the mirror. Below the level of the wash-hand basins, a row of swingy skirts, gunsmoke grey tights and brogues. Above, a row of eager faces all tinged by the same ghastly neon strip-lighting. There were earrings and beads and the odd scarf, but only one bunch of purple rosebuds. The girl suddenly felt that she would be conspicuous and looked anxiously in the mirror for approval. It took her a few moments to find her own face among the others, because the smooth complexion, the eyes startling and compelling and the glossy lips were like all the other faces copied from magazines. Only that peculiar expression, set and impassive, and the paper roses were hers and hers alone. She wanted to check her smile, but didn't dare. Decisively, she clicked her handbag shut. Then apprehensively, but affecting nonchalance, she pushed open the mauve door of the cloakroom and, with shoulders back and legs swung from the hips, she made her way to the bar.

She hurried around the dance floor, where girls in swirling skirts and Paul McCartney haircuts were showing themselves off, each dancing with her friend, without so much as a glance for the men who were already closing into pairs, in readiness for the concerted approach. There was an expression of purpose on every face, a sense of urgency in every measured move and glance.

This dancing was a serious business, taking chances and

holding back, going for looks and leaving the rest to the shouted small talk, leading questions and answers crammed into a three dance set. She knew the girls were telling lies, to the men they liked and would cling to in the slow numbers, and to the ones they didn't like and would laugh about afterwards with their girl friends. Time was short, and the hour would come when the drink would be withheld and the music stopped, too soon. It was no joke under those lights, trying to get what you wanted.

She wanted a drink, and squeezed into a gap between two high stools at the bar, squinting at the rows of bottles on the shelves. She hadn't a clue what they were or what a girl on her own ought to drink. She couldn't read the names on the bottles. She felt sick with confusion, and sat with her chin propped heavily on her fist, hoping the barman wouldn't come near her, wishing she smoked. Then she saw a face. A dark and handsome face, alive and smiling between the bottles, a real live hero of a face with long black hair and a moustache and big strong teeth that spoke to her as she stared.

'Can I buy you a drink?' She turned round, not knowing which way to look. He touched her left shoulder.

'I like your flowers.' She was pleased for he was lovely.

'I like yours,' she said.

He laughed and pressed her nose with his finger. He wasn't wearing flowers at all, but a plain black polo-neck, and long sleek black corduroy trousers. She stared. The barman was tapping his fingernails on the vinyl table top. The man in black ordered a pink gin and tonic, looked at her again, black eyebrows raised. She mustered a smile.

'I'll have a gin and tonic, please.'

She watched him steering sinuously between people and tables, carrying their two drinks. She watched the girls who eyed him greedily between mascaraed lashes, eyed her with unsugared malice as he turned again to smile. She felt honoured by his favour, purged by the glancing envy of the single girls. She felt sweet and good and smiled at him over their heads.

They sat at a table by the edge of the dancefloor, like traders at a street market, incidentally aware of the raunchy commotion in the foreground. They small-talked, sipping gin. He tipped the ash from a long cigarette and asked her with smiling expertise did she come here often.

'No,' she said, fiddling with the buttons on her cuffs, not yet, and suppressed a splutter as the gin fumes scalded her nose. He bought another, his lean finger making lines of mist on the glass. She took a sip that burnt her lips, and said she was still at school, quickly, hoping he wouldn't notice. But he never moved a muscle, said he was a bit of a scholar himself. He paused, she waited.

'At the College of Art in Belfast, actually.'

An art student. Almost an artist. She couldn't believe it. The girls at school wouldn't believe it. This noble man of wit and beauty and boundless hidden talents was hers for the taking, hers for a night. She just couldn't let this chance slip by, without taking the plunge, without falling in love. She let her knees lean dawdling towards his, until they touched. She flirted, posed and smiling, watching the birdie in his eyes. Suavely he, and she like a child with a lucky bag, dipped and fished for surprises and delights to swap, his hand on her knee, her hand on his, their faces homing in.

The band smoothly eased the tempo of the music until only a few swaying couples held the floor, watched by all the thwarted individuals standing sheepish and disheartened round the walls. She recognized faces from the crowd on the bus, men with ties slackened, thumbs in belts, they ranged in pairs, still on the prowl for their money's worth. They stalked the rows of sullen single girls perched on the benches, stiff-limbed and snappy, who sat tinned in their own sour pride, like bargains on a shelf. Special offers without takers, they watched the smooching couples swaggering into spotlit corners, while the bouncers leaned chewing by the door, sentries of moderation, checking their watches. Time was getting on.

76

'Come on, rosegirl,' said the man in black. 'Let's have the last dance.

It was a slow one. He touched the flowers, ran his finger down her breast. She wanted to grab his wrist and make it stay. He took her hand and stood up. She felt dizzy, wanton, and somehow alert. On the dance-floor she stretched up against him, her arms slack around his neck, his hair on her shoulders. They shuffled lazily against each other, the soft persuasive clothy flesh of her breasts and arms, the assertive bony hardness of him. She burrowed her face in his chest, felt his pulse bounding under the wool and bone, then his lips snuffling and foraging in her hair. Closing her eyes, she offered her mouth, coasting into a big dipper of a kiss that dissipated everything, music, dancers, the bouncers with their time-keepers, and the long road home. This was louder than loud music, brighter than bright lights, and it was all for this. The space between the floor and the roof, from one end of the dance-hall to the other was nowhere, nudged out of time and place by the smudging of their lips and tongues. He was in bed. She was on TV.

Until their teeth ground and clacked together like knives and forks in a basin, and she realized that her neck was aching from leaning backwards, and opened her eyes. Just as suddenly, the lights were up, the bouncers hustling people out the door, where they went willingly into the kindlier dark. She stood still wrapped up with him, dazed by the inquisitory lights. She looked away, embarrassed, over his shoulder at the bar where the band was knocking back pints, appraising the girls lingering among the equipment on the stage. Over his shoulder she looked, where specks of scurf glowed on his black woollen jumper.

She opened his arms, standing back from him.

'I've got to go,' she said.

He stepped forward, clamped her close.

'Stay,' he said. 'I've got a car.'

Smiling, he was unbelievable, tall, dark, and toothsome,

almost too good to be true, but real nonetheless, hard and tightly holding her. She wanted to thank him, stupidly, to kiss his fingers, to pay him for wanting her.

'No,' she said, struggling. 'I better go.'

He seemed taken aback, and loosened his hold. He took a bunch of car keys from the pocket of his trousers, jangled them swinging in front of her eyes. She watched entranced, enraptured by her predicament.

'Come with me,' he said so softly, so hard to refuse. 'I'll run you home after.'

After what, she nearly said, shook her head in time.

'I have to get my coat.' She turned without looking at him, and ran glass-slippered across the stark floor-boards to the mauve door marked 'Ladies'. She got her coat from under a chair, and hesitated in front of the mirror. Smeared and smudged, bleary with grease and sweat, the face glared back at her, affronted.

'You whore,' she mouthed, in outraged and reluctant approval of the jaded hussy in the mirror. The whore winked back. The girl pulled on her coat, dodged out of the dance-hall, across the carpark, and staidly she boarded the bus.

Quickly, it lurched forward, she found an empty seat, near the back, and with impatient fist she rubbed a keyhole in the frosted glass. And in the doorway of the dance hall, oozing smoke and light, she saw him standing cloaked and daggered, forsaken and forlorn. Under the stars and all, she thought, overwhelmed by the romance of the situation. Released from the pressure of his bodily presence, she was elated with the sorrow of their parting.

She turned right round for one lasting look through the back window, but it was spattered on the outside with mud and steamed up on the inside. The long back seat was stylishly occupied by the gentleman in the grey suit, who was inclined sheik-fashion over a prone female body, a whole row of spectators applauding his virtuosity, conducting him and counting her out. Other couples modestly discontinued and joined in acclaiming the professional touch. The man in the suit disengaged himself, inclined his head once for the audience, produced a naggin of 'Bush' from his suit pocket, took a swig and hauled the girl up beside him. She wiped her lips on the palm of her hand, and he passed her the bottle, after polishing the top with a navy handkerchief.

The bottle passed from mouth to mouth, and the dark miles drove past, measured by the occasional lights of single cars and small isolated houses edging close to the new main roads or shadowed up lanes from the old mountain roads. The passengers in the bus were settling down, the men supporting big girls on their knees, snuggling into a tired silence. Until someone glimpsed a landmark or a signpost and shouted 'Half-way home, boys, Londonderry, seventeen miles.' The crowd at the front stared at the windscreen and started off 'Oul Derry's Walls', the crowd at the back returned with 'The Sash', and the girl in the middle closed her eyes and summoned visions of her lately lost love.

'You fairly sneaked off on your man back there, didn't you?' Beery breath conspired hot against her cheek, a froggy hand clamped on her shoulder. And here was Skinner, unsteady and appealing for support.

'This seat free, miss?' She knew that he was on the scrounge for a few of the readily available home comforts of the night, but in her new-found wealth of love, matronly and generous, she patted the seat beside her, setting her face in an attitude of mature compassion. And Skinner fell for it, face down in her lap. Sniggering, almost scorching her thighs with his slow savouring breath, he stirred her feelings like gruel. She patted his head, tousling his hair with the palm of her hand, while he gurgled like a milk-sodden baby. She was moved, she wanted to cosy him, care for him, lullaby him to sleep.

'Fuck!' He chinned her lap, pulled himself up by her hair, scrambled out of the narrow seat and shuffled up the aisle. The bus stopped. The singing surged.

'Oh the seagulls have a light-house in Moville...' Skinner

retched longingly into the night. 'And they use it for a shite-house in Moville...'

Wiping the window, all concern, she saw Skinner on his knees, shuddering and spewing. She opened her handbag and took out a tissue. The bus was moving again, coloured shapes like arms waving in time to the singing. Skinner pulled himself to the back of the bus and slumped into the seat. He was pale and drained as an empty milk bottle. He let her wipe his mouth with the tissue, and settled down beside her, legs braced against the seat in front. He didn't speak, wagged his head to the beat of the singing. He was wrenching the top off a bottle, grunting quietly to himself. She resigned herself to dream and turned towards the blank window.

'Here.' He took her hand with his and closed the fingers round a bottle-neck. But warm and muscled. Her hand went limp, fell among hairs and the hot teeth of a zip.

'Hold it.' He nudged her hand with his. She gripped, felt a vein throb and sliding skin. It was soft like flesh but hard as well. It reminded her of something she had felt when they were dancing. She hadn't mentioned it then, and she couldn't look now. She tried to think, to work it all out, surely and sensibly, but was overcome by a panic close to exaltation. She calmed herself with embarrassment, and sternly considered the situation. She did not know this man at all, and it was obvious that she was now involved in a scene of some intimacy with a complete stranger.

'What do you do?' she asked him politely.

'Pull.' he said, curling his fingers and squeezing her hand.

She was affronted. The matter in hand here was something nice as butchery. Doherty's porkers had nothing on this. It was hot as a Cookstown banger, sizzling fit to burst its skin, the warm peeled feel of a soft boiled egg. But worse, it lived and pulsed like the scraggy throat of a chicken near to the end of its terror. She would have pardoned gladly, craved the sanction to desist. What were the others doing? He would surely take offence, might turn nasty. Besides, this was a chance in a million, to have it out with ignorance, to be prepared for when it mattered. It might even get better as you went along. She was grateful for the high-backed seclusion of the seats. The thought of being caught at this lark flushed her with fear. Hot red light blinded her sensibilities, curiosity killing the cat of caution, caution clawing at conscience, and a snake on the loose. She clenched her eyes shut, loosening her grip. He squeezed her fingers, pawing her hand into motion. She strained away from him, leaning close against the cold night-swept window of the bus. Her hand was still there, but not her's, someone else's, his.

'No,' she whispered.

'No,' she said, in a voice like a shout.

'No,' she breathed, and a half-moon of mist marked the glass, condensed to a light drive of droplets, evaporated.

Stamping and cheering, as the lights went on, the bus-driver had had enough. The singers coughed, blinked. The couples came up for air, shifting and giggling, laughing through their noses. In her clammy hand there was a slackening, a gentle subsidence. She heard a zip pulled.

'Brewer's droop,' said Skinner, irrepressibly cheerful.

Uncomprehending, she turned her back on him and all shortcomings, concentrating instead on the boldly brazen image of this new experience. Bad words failed her.

In the streaming window of the bus she saw her face unmasked, wide-eyed and a mouth full of crab-apple, the rest a blur. She didn't look at him or speak to him again.

She made her own way home, alone. She undressed without putting on the light, carelessly. Shoes first, her feet aching for release. Tights and skirt and smock, zips only half undone. A pin stung her finger. Bloody roses. She felt for them, searching with her fingers. She shook the smock, scrabbled half-heartedly in the heap on the floor. It smelt of cigarettes and deodorised sweat. But no roses. Too tired to bother, she had other things to think of, lying on her back in the dark.

'Did you have a nice night?' Her mother looked in, already

glad for her, recalling her own ration of foxtrots and quick-steps, tea and Paris buns.

'Very nice,' she mumbled back, and blushed beneath the sheets. And wondered in a sudden flush of sorrow where they lay, the long-stemmed man in black, and blank-eyed Skinner with his secret bloom. And wondered then, in the same flush of sorrow, where she had lost them, her own roses, dusty purple and sweet with the smell of promise. She almost laughed. They were a small price to have paid for such a night to remember, for such memories and revelations.

'It wasn't a bad night,' she thought. 'Not bad at all, for a beginner.'

And smiling smugly, she snuggled into sleep. But in her dreams some other girl was scouring the scratch-grained floor of a vacant dance-hall, picking with frozen fingers through the grit and gravel in a deserted carpark, leant on grubby knees and hands, straining under the seats of an empty bus, feeling fag-ends and paper hankies and crumpled bottle tops for stems, for leaves.

scene around six

Eileen Pollock

Belfast. Royal Avenue. Five p.m. Rush hour.

Quickly, pick a person, any person. . . That one!

Henry John Shiels, about fifty, ex-machine tool operator.

Quickly, quickly, pick another, any other . . . There! That woman.

Rose McCusker, early forties, mother of five.

Good.

'I know you people must get about a lot, but have you ever been to Malta, Captain?' said Henry John, three pints into the evening.

'Malta?' said the Englishman, wondering whether to bother. . . 'No', he decided, 'one place I've never been to, actually, Malta. They say it's a lovely place.'

'Oh, a lovely place, a lovely place,' said Henry John. Beautiful beaches. I went there last year. Oh yes. Eight o'clock in the morning I arrived. Straight onto the beach. Sun beating down. Water glinting. Gorgeous! Set up the deckchair, slapped on the suntan lotion, got the knotted hankie on the head, and settled down to soak it all up, full of poetry and well-being . . . You know the way?'

'Um', said the Captain, who quite frankly didn't. This public relations business was all very well, he was thinking, but what he wouldn't give for a pint of Ruddles.

'The dark eleventh hour

Draws on and sees us sold . . .

To every evil power

We fought against of old . . . I love a good poem

Rebellion, rapine, hate

Oppression, wrong and greed

Are loosed to rule our fate

By England's act and deed . . . no offence meant, Captain, only an oul' poem', said Henry John, very hail-fellow-well-met. 'Suddenly', he went on, 'Suddenly! A familiar voice booms in my ear . . . "Henry John!" it said, "Fancy you being here! . . " . . . and dammit to hell if it wasn't my ex-boss Major Phillips. "Sure, Major", I says, "You've been recommending this here Malta place till us for so long, I thought I'd take a chance on it myself when the oul' compensation came through." He goes there every year, like.' He took a swig of his Guinness, waiting for the inevitable.

'Compensation?' asked the Captain dutifully.

'Aye. £200 I got. Compensation. For that there.' He solemnly waved a crumpled black-gloved hand in front of the Captain's startled face and wheezed in delight at the Captain's dismay. 'Done that in a machine so I did. £200 worth that there . . . Oh aye, and the wee clock they gave me for long service . . . "Despite the fact you brought your working relationship with the company to a close rather more abruptly than good manners would normally allow, eh, Henry John, heh-heh-heh!" as your man put it . . . Major Phillips! Aye, used to be my commandant in the B-Specials too before they were disbanded, of course, but I refuse to talk about that now, or I'll just get upset. Will you have another, Captain? What am I talking about, of course you will two more pints here,

Sammie, if you wouldn't mind. . . He's a UDR man now of course. Major Phillips. Great military man'.

Henry John paid carefully for the two pints. 'Not tremendous on personnel relations, but. He says to me, "Did you never think of joining up yourself yet, Henry John?" he says. Talk about spoiling your holiday! So I just said to him, dignified like, "They said I wasn't suitable, sir." You know? And then what does he say? "Still," he says, "you're a lucky man" . . . "Pardon?" I says. "You're a lucky man," he says. "Look at Alice Smith, there, sure she got chewed to death by her machine and nobody even knew until two hours after it happened! Tell me, are you right-handed, by any chance, Henry John?" he sais.'

'And are you?' asked the Captain, with respect.

Henry John looked at him with great amusement. 'Not any more!' he cackled.

'Listen to this,' said Rosie. ' "Warm the brandy, set it alight and pour it over the pigeons!. . ." '

She looked up from the magazine and turned to her neighbour in the waiting room.

'Do you ever feel you don't exist? Eh? You know, without being metaphysical about it nor nothing, do you? Sometimes I am reminded of when I was a wee girl, standing in a shop waiting to be served, and all these big people getting served before me till eventually I'd begin to wonder did I have a face at all?' She turned to the magazine. 'Look at that! . . . "Wash and peel the figs . . ." '

'The what?' said the other woman.

'You might well ask,' said Rosie. 'The figs. . . figs.'

'Oh, aye,' said the woman, not wanting to show her ignorance, but fairly convinced all the same that you'd want to peel the cellophane off them first before you washed them, even supposing you wanted to wash them.

'I mean,' said Rosie, mostly to herself, 'As far as I was ever concerned, I thought the idea was simply that you fed them up, you made them big and strong, and then they would get a good job. Now there's no jobs to be had and I seriously begin to wonder why I bother.'

'Is your husband not working, missus?' said the other woman.

'My husband? No, he's dead, my husband.'

'Oh,' said the woman, looking for clues to help her compose her face right.

'Aye, what is it now? Eight months ago, it must be, he died. Charlie. That was his name.'

'Charlie.'

'Aye,' Rosie nodded, fondly. Then she remembered. 'D'you see my neighbour, but? Wait till you hear this. . . she says to me after, "Och, I suppose youse are all regretting that *fight* youse were having that morning before he left? I could hear yez at it," she says, and she's sniggering like . . . snigger, snigger . . . "Och, that there must have been the last time you seen him alive!" she says. Would you credit it? Eh?' Rosie snorted in disgust, and the other woman shook her head in commiseration.

'I remember it, like,' she went on. 'It was our Michael had started it. That's my son, Michael . . . "Tactics," he was shouting, "Tactics is one thing, defeatism is another."

"I am not talking about defeatism," says Charlie, "But you can't coerce a million screaming Prods into a republic they do not want."

"I'm not talking about coercion," says Michael, "I'm talking about an end to coercion, and if you can't see the difference, if you call *that* coercion, you need your head examined," he says. "It's no wonder you can't get a bloody job!"

'Well that's enough for me. "Don't you dare speak to your father like that," I says. I can't abide disrespect in a child. "You don't know the half of what that man has been through to keep this here family fed and clothed," I says. "There's women in this street have to steal their housekeeping out of their man's pockets when he comes home plastered on pay night," I says. "Because if they didn't do that they might never see it at all . . . I have never had to do that," I says. "Never. Your father comes home here," I says, "Hands me over my money, and sits down to tea with his family. Then he goes out and gets plastered." I says!'

Rosie dissolved in peals of laughter.

'Well,' she said finally, composing herself again, laughter subsiding, 'I never knew your woman was listening in to all this, see!' She finished enjoying her joke, and went quiet for a bit.

'Hmph!' she frowned. 'So I says to her, this neighbour, "I do not indeed regret that there," I says. "I'll tell you what I do regret," I says. "I regret the fact, for example, that my husband lived and *died* and never had a decent house to live in." And this here is the irony of it,' said Rosie, turning to the other woman. 'Do you know what his trade was?'

'What was that?'

'He was a bricklayer! Aye.' Rosie laughed quietly. 'Been out of work for ten years.' She picked up the magazine again. 'That's what I regret.'

'Okay then,' said Martha, laying the table with measured wrath. 'Seeing as how you're so well acquainted with him, are you going to go round and ask him about it?' Silence. 'Are you listening to me, Henry John?'

'Two big women in the house,' grumbled Henry John from behind the rustling *Telegraph*. 'Two big women in the house and no tea yet. What have you been doing with yourselves, I'd like to know? And what's that lassie doing snivelling in the kitchen anyway?'

'Leave her alone, she's upset. And stop trying to avoid the issue. Are you going to speak to him or are you not? Are you?'

'What's upset her now? Or am I not allowed to know as

usual?'

Martha paused. Should she tell him? Yes, might as well get it over with. 'Don't be hard on her, now, Henry John, she's not done anything wrong, and it came to her as a terrible shock, poor wee lamb, but . . . ah . . . she's been given her notice, Henry John. Now don't be angry.'

'She has what? She has what? Terrible shock, indeed! Sure I could have told her she wouldn't last. Putting her on the picture counter! It's not as if she was even the slightest bit *artistic*, that wee girl couldn't draw breath. . .'

'I heard that!' roared Sadie's voice rising through her sobs in the kitchen. 'I heard that . . . and . . . and you've . . .' But she choked with rage and collapsed into tears again.

'Would you just hold your horses and stop jumping to con-clusions!' hissed Martha. 'That is not what happened at all. It appears they all went in today and found the whole place in a fluster because the Big Chief Managing Director from England had arrived for a bit of an inspection, for to see why they weren't pulling in his 37½% profit he says he has to have. Did you know Henry John, every day they all got issued with sales performance sheets for the same day last year, the whole lot of them and if they didn't continually top them figures by the right amount they were in serious bother. Now I didn't know that, but that there is a fact..

'So anyway, there's our Sadie, and she has got herself all dolled up and all for to look charming and beautiful and all for his Supreme Managership, and he comes round and he points to this picture and he says, "What about that one there?" And our Sadie says, "Sure you couldn't give that one away, sir!" You know, laughing and joking and gushing all over him, like. "My dear young lady," he says, "I'll have you know I was the sales representative who sold that picture to this shop five years ago, and if I can sell it to you, you can sell it to somebody else!" Och, she was ragin', so she was, Henry John. And she had wasted half a bottle of perfume on him and all. And it didn't mean the slightest difference, they were still told at half past four that the firm would be pulling out next month. What do you think of that. Henry John?'

Henry John folded his paper, tight-lipped. 'That's your multinationals for you,' he said grimly. How many times had he said it? It made him heart-sore, to tell you the truth. 'That's the way it is these days. You have no protection. Nothing ⁄ . . Sadie!' he called 'C'mere, love, and tell us all about it.'

'Oh look, talking of protection again, Henry John,' said Martha taking advantage of the mellowed atmosphere. 'Would you not go round and see your friend there, would you not?'

Henry John glowered. 'Maybe I will and maybe I won't,' he said. 'Has that wee girl still not got my tea ready? . . . Sadie!'

'Next!'

'That's you,' said the other man to Rosie.

Rosie gathered herself together, shopping bags, parcels, handbag, gloves and all and went through the frosted glass door.

'Evening, Brian,' she beamed, closing the door behind her and going over to the counter. 'Is this the housing department?' She hesitated before taking her seat.

The man behind the counter looked up from his papers to eye her with suspicion. 'Yes, Mrs. McCusker, this is the housing department.'

'Great. Any sign of a house?' She sat down, arranging all round her.

'Name?'

'Mrs. Rose McCusker,' she said, very matter-of-fact. She did this every week.

'Address?'

'Chez Nous, Windahmeeyah Pork, Churryvelley. . ."

Brian successfully created a pained silence. Then replied: 'Mrs. McCusker I think you'll find progress a little less elusive if you refrain from departing from the facts. Thank you.'

'Listen dear, I don't have to make anything up. The naked truth leaves very little room for exaggeration. 23, Talbot Street, Falls Road.'

'Your husband is dead?'

'Yes.'

'What was his occupation?'

'Unemployed.' Rosie watched him write it down. 'Well . . . that wasn't his profession, you understand, but it certainly occupied more of his time than anything else.'

'Number of children?'

'Only the five.' She smiled. 'Same as last week.' The sort of smile that curdles milk.

'One son in jail, is this correct?' stabbed Brian, with studied professional disinterest.

'This is correct,' replied Rosie, perfectly nonplussed. 'He was convicted of burying guns in our back garden.'

Half of Brian's brain thought, 'Typical,' as the other half thought, 'I don't want to know this; this has nothing to do with me.' Meanwhile his voice said, 'I see,' just to fill in space. Pause.

'We haven't got a back garden, Brian. And that there is in fact what I wanted to talk to you about. I want a house with four bedrooms, one bathroom, one inside toilet, no leaks, hot and cold water and a garden. Now.'

'Mrs. McCusker, I don't think there is a single person in this building who is not aware of the fact that Mrs. Rose McCusker of 23, Talbot Street, Falls Road, wants a house with four bedrooms, one bathroom, one inside toilet, no leaks, hot and cold water, and, thank you for reminding me, a garden. Now. You are equally aware of the fact that your name is down on the housing list to that effect and that we will inform you as soon as a suitable house is available, and when your turn comes, and that there is no need whatsoever for you to persist in this weekly pantomime. Mrs. McCusker.'

'Poleglass, Brian.'

I must have done something dreadful in a previous

existence, thought Brian, carefully redirecting his churning aggression into a stony-faced flights of the imagination. The very fact of Rose McCusker had already convinced him, several weeks ago, that there might be something in the theory of reincarnation after all. He had decided that nobody could get that stubborn in one lifetime.

'What about the proposed 4,000 houses out at Poleglass there? Come on, Brian, put us down for one of them. That there would be dead handy for me, just up the road like that, tucked in between my sister-in-law in Andersonstown and the brother out at Twinbrooke. Eh?'

Here we go, thought Brian. 'It is unlikely that 4,000 houses will be built at Poleglass,' he said, trying to sound as if he were saying something like, "Have another bun, Vicar".

'Why not?'

'The planning department has not confirmed the need for them to be built yet.'

'Brian, I am one of 600,000 people living in substandard housing.'

No reaction. 'Actually, I am one of the 300,000 people living in a house unfit for human habitation.' Nothing. Grimly she gathered her belongings and stood. 'Who do I speak to in the planning department?'

'Mrs. McCusker. Please sit down. Houses *are* being built. We just have to be careful where we put them, that is all.'

'Pardon?'

'It has simply been brought to the attention of the planning department by certain people at present holding office on the council in question, Mrs. McCusker, that the linking of Andersonstown and Twinbrooke estates by another estate housing the overflow from West Belfast would only, and I quote: "serve to create a solid working-class Roman Catholic ghetto the whole way out to Twinbrooke, a hot-bed of republican discontent and a threat to security and law and order". Now, Mrs. McCusker, would you or would you not say there is some sense in refusing to create the very breeding

91

grounds for violence and discontent?'

'A lot of sense, Brian. And if you don't see me rehoused fairly soon you're going to get the full benefit of my own personal violence and discontent, Republican or otherwise, right here in this office.'

'Is that a threat, Mrs. McCusker?'

'No,' said Rosie, her hand on the door. 'That's a promise.'

There was nothing for it, thought Henry John. So he put on his coat, cap and scarf and dragged himself round to see the Captain. Three quarters of the way there he was already in a huff again, thinking to himself: 'You tell a person you've had a casual drink with someone and all of a sudden you're supposed to be bosom buddies.' So by the time he'd got poked and prodded and searched down at the barracks, he was in a lovely mood. 'It's disgusting,' he thought, 'Humiliating. You're trying to do your civic duty like a decent citizen and they make you feel like a criminal.'

'Henry John,' said the Captain, 'And what can we do for you?' ('I'd met him down at the club the odd time, see,' Henry John explained in the pub after.)

'We demand protection, Sir,' said Henry John. 'At the bottom of our street. The Fe. . . the Roman Catholics over the way have started restoring some of the bricked up houses on their side of no-man's land there, and . . . ah . . . we're a bit worried about this obvious. . . ah. . . southerly encroach-ment . . . (good man, Henry John, he thought to himself, give it to him in military terms, that's right) . . . southerly encroachment on our lives and liberties, with the attendant future possibility of marauding Catholic bands attacking our defenceless women and children, like. We'd like a wee wall built at the end of our street to protect our families. Sir.'

The Captain frowned a moment in silence. 'I seem to remember, Henry John,' he said slowly, 'Those houses were in fact bricked up because the Roman Catholic population were having to flee in some consternation from marauding Protestant bands.'

('Well,' said Henry John later to his open-mouthed audience in the pub, 'You could have knocked me down with a fart. I was *stunned,* so I was.')

'Am I to understand, Sir,' he said coldly, 'That the god-fearing people who sent me here in good faith have once again got to resort to bodily defending themselves against the possibility of attack by the enemies of the state, as they have had to do time and time again? When a wee wall would do the job?'

'We'll see what we can do,' said the Captain, showing him out.

'Do you know how much money is spent on defence every year, Sammie?'

'I don't indeed,' said Sammie.

'£2,000 million is spent on defence every year. Do you know what we got?'

'What?'

'Four large concrete flower pots full of daffodils.' Henry John nodded sadly over his Guinness. 'Oh, I went back. I went back and I says could they not send us round a few radar controlled ground-to-air geraniums, for the daffodils wasn't even keeping out the dirty flies from their stinking Fenian kitchens! A bunch of daffodils between life and death! And we're talking here about the best bloody army in the world!'

Belfast. Royal Avenue. Seven p.m. Nobody around.

Another jeepful of soldiers sleeks by in the rain. One of them shot John Boyle.

underwear

Mary Rose Callaghan

'Hello,' Rita said into the phone, 'this is the Superior.'

'Are you the Reverend Mother?' a man's voice asked.

Parents, she sighed. 'I am the Superior, yes.'

'This is Alan Murray, manager of Dooley's in Henry Street. Eh-- look, there's someone here dressed up as one of your nuns.'

'If this is some sort of joke, I'm hang. . .'

'Oh, it's no joke,' he said, laughing. 'She claims to be Sister Margaret Mary Becker.'

'But Sister *is* one of our nuns! Why do you think she's dressed up?'

'You'd better come in, so.'

She kept her voice level. 'Just tell me the problem. I'm far too bus. . .'

'The problem,' he said icily, 'is that Sister was apprehended leaving this shop with items of underwear she didn't pay for. And if you don't come in, I'll be forced to call the guards.'

Her face felt on fire. 'I'll be right in. Give me half-an-hour. But there must be some mistake.'

'Good, I'll wait so.'

'Ah— it might take longer. The traffic.' She cleared her throat and continued firmly, 'The convent will, of course, pay for anything Sister bought.'

Click. The line went dead. Rita replaced the receiver and paused by the hall window-sill. Maggy May? The little ones doted on the flabby old infirmarian, trailed her everywhere. This morning when that spindly-legged child fainted at Mass, she was first over and carried her out, whispering wheezily, 'That's my pet, my girl.'

The convent buzzed at the faintest hint of gossip. Good thing she came to the phone herself. The less said, and no recriminations. Maggy May would see a psychiatrist. But, underwear?

Car keys were needed now. Cheque book. Outside it was rainy and almost dark. Lapland, with those wintry trees. But no time to go to her cell for a coat.

Abruptly she turned and the green baize screen clattered onto the floor. Useless, but the old nuns insisted. Lifting it, she was suddenly queasy from the smell of floor wax. It permeated the house, along with incense, chalk, cabbagy dinners. She sighed, steadied the screen, then hurried through the mossy gloom to the bursar's office.

Sister Clement was dwarfed by a huge oak desk.

'Is anything wrong?'

'No.' Rita met her watery gaze. 'I just want the car keys. Anyone out?'

'Only Margaret Mary,' the older nun sighed, reaching for the keys. 'She went into town to collect her glasses.'

'I'll be out for an hour. Give me the cheque book. Or do you have cash? About twenty pounds?'

'Wouldn't a cheque do?'

'Don't you have cash?'

'Yes, but it's awkward. I've made out the lodgment slips.'

'A cheque might be difficult. Give me cash as you've got it.'

Sister's bloodless lips curved downwards as she pulled open

95

the desk drawer. 'The Lopez man paid this morning. In notes. Bet it's counterfeit. What comes of taking every Tom, Dick. . .

'Whose is this?' Idly Rita picked up a brown ornamental puppy from the desk. Yellow tears splashed down his cherubic face onto his chubby paws. 'I miss you' was in large red letters on the base.

Sister smiled slowly. 'It's Gary. God bless him!'

'Gary?' Rita frowned. That stupid little yapper she insisted be put down.

'Margaret Mary dropped him. But I've got a good glue . . .' She pushed four fivers across the desk. 'Is it a bill?'

Pope Pius XII glared suspiciously from his portrait on the wall. Surely time for a successor? 'You might send a message to 6A,' Rita said. 'Tell them to carry on.'

Speeding down the drive, she waved to the gardener hoeing by the massive gates. Hard to imagine that in the novitiate he had chauffered them everywhere. Still, happy days, a gaggle of girls flapping round the grounds after tea, with rambling blackberries everywhere, and angry swans attacking anything in trousers. Now the swans were gone, the male eaten by a fox, and the female pined away. Only one novice in two years, the choir never sang the *Benedictus,* and sickly ribbons of white houses sprawled on the lower hockey field.

After the village, she accelerated for the long stretch before the shopping centre. Friday evening's mad rush would catch her coming back. Tonight she must phone her father about his arthritis. Recently it was worse, but on her last visit he had brushed her off. 'Ah, don't worry about that me child. Amn't I almost with herself?'

Hypocrisy!

Later he'd said, 'Child, would ye not wear the veil?'

Why did he still upset her? He didn't drink now. And her brother said he boasted that she was Superior at thirty-six. Hmn, no matter. She could never forgive him her childhood. Never. She could see him now, redfaced and eyes bulging.

'The bitch is gone! Left me with six brats! And I didn't

96

want one of ye! Not one of ye!' He swerved drunkenly, children and dogs scattering.

Poor Mama, married to that.

And at sober breakfasts, when he had to be up to teach, the children ate in strained silence, with him shakily sipping tea. But someone would be picked on before the day was out.

'Look at this room! What? Cheek me wouldye? Get me the strap!'

Then screams followed by the swish and smack of leather.

Once he had seen her chatting to a boy from the college and dragged her home crying.

'Hussy! Is this what the nuns teach you? Is this what they do with my money? My eldest daughter going to bad! Over my dead body! My dead body!'

Rita braked for the lights at the end of George's Street. Going to the bad. Honestly. Oh, if he'd been drunk she could forgive it. But he was off it for Lent. He had no control, picking all Mama's tulips after her funeral, and strewing them on the gravel.

'Twenty-nine! Thirty! Thirty-one! Thirty-one! Thirty-one! Only . . .'

He stopped, and fell on the earth, clawing it.

Whitefaced, Rita gathered the wilting heads. 'Mama's tulips. Mama's tulips.'

'What? Here! Give me . . .' He grabbed the flowers and scrunched them into the earth. 'Look! That's where your mother is!'

When she said she was entering he quipped, 'One less to feed!' And he didn't look up from his newspaper.

'But who'll make porridge?' her little sister asked.

Later she found her brother sobbing in the toilet.

'I'm not going far. Now stop! Please stop! There'll be holidays. You can visit!'

A giant christmas tree lit the pillars of the newly washed Bank of Ireland. Childhood, Christmas lights, funny how it all

97

came back. They had made most of their presents. The big event was Midnight Mass, then walking home through the inky night. *Come follow Me and I will be your God.*

She felt nothing in the chapel now. Nothing touched her, not even the books she read. Nothing. Still, she worked at her book, belonged to a women's political group, humoured the old nuns. And she slogged for the Leaving Class, helped them understand poetry. No one bothered over her. Her father had once slammed shut her copy of *The Wasteland*. 'Poetry! Ha! It doesn't even rhyme!'

What did he recite in his cups?

'Alas for the rarity,
 Of Christian Charity - -.'

How did the rest go? He always finished with 'Under the green sod lies.'

At O'Connell Bridge, she waited for the guard's signal to move on. Was she wrong about Gary? Maggy May had loved him but he yapped at everyone else's ankles. One bite meant trouble. An amiable dog, that would stay outside might've been different.

Then the reprieve. In the bus, on the way to the Dog's Home, Maggy May had met Mrs. Farrell, a housewife who agreed to take him. Now they phoned each other daily, or, if Mrs. Farrell was on holidays, the convent was flooded with telegrams.

'New dogfood suits.'

Or, 'Has found little friend.'

Or, 'Is enjoying sea air.'

Weird. That time waiting for the phone Maggy May had muttered, 'Ah, Mother, the Lord punishes those He loves.' She shook her head sadly.

'They left him alone all day yesterday! God help him! I knew he'd be desperate so I waited outside. . .'

'In this weather?' Rita had kept a straight face.

'But didn't he see me and bark through the window!' She smiled and went off murmuring, 'The Lord punishes. . .'

Town was crowded. Lights winked magically on the trees lining the centre of O'Connell Street. Clery's looked almost continental with new bright yellow canopies over the windows. Why didn't Maggy May get her underwear there, on account? The old nuns weren't used to modern shops, still wore the habit, couldn't adapt to being ordinary people.

She parked behind Roches Stores and weaved her way towards Henry Street. There, mothers with wailing children, pushed parcels in prams, girls linked happily, street traders shouted and waved balloons, everyone pushed. She had her nieces and nephews to shop for, but was this getting and spending all it meant? And what was this man's name? He sounded so sure of himself. The children, even the parents, were in awe of her. But a store manager? Who insisted Maggy May had stolen?

At Dooley's a salesgirl pointed her to a door marked 'Manager's Office'. She knocked and a burly young man came out and looked enquiringly at her smart tweed suit.

'I'm Mother Rita,' she said walking in. Maggy May sat in one corner bent over a hanky. Briefly their eyes met.

He laughed and held out his hand. 'I was expecting a nun.'

'I am a nun,' Rita said, shaking hands and taking in the several pairs of frothy panties on the green formica topped desk. A skimpy bra cascaded down one side.

He pulled out a chair. 'Sister, a seat. Ha! You can't tell who anyone is these days!'

Rita opened her handbag. 'Thank you, I'd rather stand. How much do they come to? We must be getting back.'

He waved away a uniformed figure appearing in the doorway. The door closed and he pointed again to a chair. 'A seat,' he said, smiling with his mouth.

Rita held out two five pound notes. 'This should cover it.'

'I'm afraid it's not so simple.' He held up a pair of panties. 'Sister was apprehended leaving the shop with these items.'

'I'm sure she meant to pay for them.'

He dropped the incriminating garment. 'Hmm. Well, I'm

not so sure! She didn't have the money. And she could hardly wear them!'

Rita ignored his smirk. He planted his palms heavily on the desk and leant towards her. 'In this shop we fight a constant war against shop-lifters. And when we catch them we can make it hot!' He gestured towards the old nun. 'Sister, here, is a nun. She should know the difference between right and wrong.'

Maggy May began to sob. Rita looked over helplessly. 'It's surely not just a case of right and wrong,' she said after a second.

'What did you say?'

'That some things are not just a case of right and wrong.'

His eyes were an incredulous blue. 'But if *nuns* do it!'

'She's no different because she wears a uniform.'

'Ah! So you admit she's not different from other people?'

'Yes, yes, I do.'

'Well, then?' He folded his arms triumphantly. 'Why should she be treated different?'

'I . . . ah . . .'

'Take yourself now. You don't want to be treated different!'

She caught his appraising glance. 'Why do you say that?'

'Well, your clothes.'

She let the remark float over her.

'Can't you see she's an old woman?'

'Ha! Age! We have them all ages! All ages!'

Rita groped for the chair and sank into it. He sat down too, folded his arms and stared at her quizzically. Maggy May wheezed noisily.

At last he picked up the phone. 'Send me in a bag and a receipt for four pounds fifty pence.' He looked at Rita. 'You'll take charge of Sister? You'll guarantee this won't happen again?'

'Of course.' She put the money on the table.

When the salesgirl came in with the bag he told her to

bring back the change. Then slowly he folded the garments and put them one by one in the bag. 'I wanted you to realise the seriousness of the situation. I know she's a nun, but next time . . .'

'Yes!' Rita said. 'Yes!'

Hastily she pulled up Maggy May and steered her out to the white light of the shop. It was closing time and a cluster of salesgirls stared as they made for the door.

Outside the old nun stopped abruptly. 'Mother. . .'

Rita pushed her gently onwards. 'You don't have to say anything.

'I just couldn't stop thinking of him — that's . . .'

Rita sighed guiltily. 'Yes, Gary, I know.'

'Ah, now Mother — A boy I knew. Long, long ago.'

'A boy *you* knew!'

'Ah, yes, Mother. . .' The old eyes hazed over. 'We'd go up the fields together, and lie in the long grass and the cows would come and gape at our nakedness. Sometimes. . .'

'Stop it! Do you hear me? Stop it!' Rita shook the old woman's arm.

'You'll never go out alone again! Do you hear me? Do you hear me?'

'Yes!' The old woman sobbed. 'Yes!'

Rita plunged frantically into the crowd with the old nun tottering after. At the car she fumbled shakily for her keys, and glancing over the top, saw Maggy May pale and hunched in the rain. Good God, what was the point of being in a convent? Of slogging for other people's children? If she made an old woman cry?

'What was his name?' she asked, when they joined the snake of traffic sliding homewards through the dark.